Copyright

The unauthorized reproduction or distribution of a copyrighted work is illegal. Criminal copyright infringement, including infringement without monetary gain, is investigated by the FBI and is punishable by fines and federal imprisonment.

Please purchase only authorized editions and do not participate in or encourage, the piracy of copyrighted material. Your support of author's rights is appreciated.

This book is a work of fiction. Names, characters, places and incidents are the products of the author's imagination or used fictitiously. Any resemblance to actual events, locales or persons, living or dead is entirely coincidental.

Complication copyrighted 2022 by Delta James

Editing: Lori White Creative Editing Services

Cover Design: Dar Albert, Wicked Smart Designs

✽ Created with Vellum

COMPLICATION

SYNDICATE MASTERS: NORTHERN LIGHTS

DELTA JAMES

For Chris, Renee and the Girls:
Who make my life so much easier and better

Acknowledgements:
Editing: Lori White Creative Editing Services
Cover Design: Dar Albert, Wicked Smart Designs

PROLOGUE

Freyja listened to the other gods bicker over petty differences. How could they ever bring peace and prosperity to those who worshipped them if they continued to squabble like greedy children? Ragnarök was coming. She needed to ensure those left behind would be protected.

Stroking the fur of the blue gray cat in her lap, she rose from her seat and removed herself from the great hall. The cat trotted off to join his brother. The two shifted from their common origins into the ice lion and the snow leopard before joining Freyja, who looked to the great boar often depicted with her. He, too, shifted and became the winter tiger.

. . .

"Hear me now. The gods continue to argue amongst themselves even as Ragnarök approaches. I bestow upon you three the gift of transfiguration. From beast to man, you and your descendants will be able to shape shift at will. Live among the people as human, calling upon your shifted form to lend you strength when it is needed. Watch over my people and see they do not perish from this earth."

The beasts exchanged looks with one another, their humanity already visible. As one, they emitted a soft roar, accepting their gift. Their destiny.

CHAPTER 1

Sabu Stronghold
Bergen, Norway
Five Years After Present Day

Anders Jensen waited in the darkest corner of his bedchamber. Anticipation and need were powerful aphrodisiacs. For many years he had been forced to watch from the shadows while others controlled those around him. When his moment had come to seize power, he had done so—ruthlessly, efficiently, and completely. But now he waited for the arrival of his prey: Gabriella.

The creak in the floorboard just outside the master's chambers alerted him to the fact she was near. The second the door cracked open; he could feel her trepidation tinged with the sweet scent of her arousal. She glanced around the room, but he'd had many years to learn and practice the art of fading into the darkness—unseen, undetected, unstoppable.

Gabriella went about getting undressed and readying herself for bed. He could feel her confusion and concern traveling down the ethereal tether that stretched between them. He kept his own feelings to himself, not allowing them to travel down the link. She knew he was supposed to return this evening from a meeting held in secret between the leaders of the Northern Lights Coalition. After far too many Aquavits and one too many Cuban cigars, they had reached the momentous decision to never again be parted from their mates.

Anders had taken great care not to be seen by anyone at the castle. His efforts had shown him a few weaknesses in their defenses. Perhaps weakness was too strong a word. He doubted anyone but he or one of his ranking clan members would be able to utilize the information, but still, nothing that made their stronghold impenetrable could be a bad thing.

Sabu Stronghold sat high atop the cliffs overlooking Bergen, Norway. The Jensen family had held the fortress since before the Battle of Hastings in Great Britain. 1066 had marked the last incursion of the Norwegian Vikings into Britain... at least the last one they admitted to. Some said the Nazis had forced an exodus of more than five hundred Norwegians to Scotland during WWII, with three hundred seventy-three taking the *Shetland Bus*, but still others had made the perilous journey unbeknownst to anyone. Their histories had been lost in the mists of time, unrecorded, unremembered by anyone other than those closest to them.

Once Gabriella had settled herself naked in bed, Anders moved silently and slipped up onto the mattress without being detected. When he clasped his hand over her mouth, her hazel eyes flew open, and she followed the line of his arm up to peer over her shoulder and lock eyes with his. Her heartbeat and breathing both increased in rhythm.

"Stay still. The door to your bedchamber is locked and the stone walls are thick. No one can hear you scream. You are mine and there is nothing you can do to prevent me from taking what I am due. Do you understand?" She nodded. "Serve me well and you may yet live to see the sunrise."

He removed his hand from her mouth to quickly render himself naked—her eyes riveted to his fully engorged cock as it jutted away from his body. He leaned over her, replacing his hand with a brutal kiss. The predator was loose and meant to take what was his. There was no need to hold back. Gabriella was strong and fearless. She feared no man and could endure any of the ways he chose to make use of her glorious body. Anders growled low in his throat, and she made an answering noise. Tearing his mouth away, he took a breath before fusing his lips back to hers, tongue plunging into the deepest recesses of her mouth to taste and plunder, pillage and savor. After all, he came from a long line of Vikings—plundering and pillaging was one of the things his ancestors did best.

As if to echo their passion, flash lightning lit the inky night sky followed by a bolt of nature's electricity and a roll of angry thunder. The sky lit up with a different kind of energy—the Aurora Borealis made one of its rare appearances in the skies over Bergen. The phenomenon was more common further north, but as his people had always believed they were a manifestation of their Nordic gods, Anders took it as a sign that the gods blessed his treatment of this woman. The thunder clapped again, urging him to take what was his, to possess and reclaim the sexy art historian/lawyer who had fallen under his control.

Pressing her into the mattress, Anders covered Gabriella with his body, forcing her thighs apart as he settled himself between them. He stretched her arms over her head, capturing them with one hand while he used the other to palm her breast, rolling her nipple between his thumb and forefinger. Crushing his lips to hers, his hand trailed down her body, callused fingers that touched, explored, and teased every centimeter of the skin he encountered. It felt like refined silk, contrasting with the pebbled texture of her stiffened nipples.

His fingers slid between her legs, splaying her labia, bypassing her clit to draw her honeyed essence from her molten core to coat her outer lips and clit. No matter what she said when the sun rose, she would not be able to deny her desire for his possession. The wealth of her slick was more than enough proof of her need.

His thick, hard cock throbbed, probing and seeking her entrance. Finding it, Anders pressed inside her in a single pass, making her shudder and cry out as she squirmed, seeking to free herself from his savage embrace. Gabriella's body arched and she snarled as her orgasm washed over her, consuming her in a way that left her breathless and even more aroused. He found it curious that one of the things he liked best—that she often climaxed just from his possession—was something that irritated her to no end.

Pulling back until he was almost uncoupled from her, Anders slammed back into her, burying his face in her neck as he began to pound into her, reveling in the feel of her writhing beneath him. He had timed this perfectly. She was ripe for plunder and as he continued to hammer her pussy, she gave over and surrendered to him. This was the moment he always waited for, and he released her wrists, slipping his hands under her buttocks, cupping them to keep her still while he took his due and had his fill.

Anders growled and thrust into her again and again—each time seemingly more ferocious than the last. Gabriella's legs came up, angling her body to ease his penetration, her arms winding around him, fingers flexing into his back as she chewed on his clavicle. This woman was made for passion and pleasure, and he meant to take her full measure.

"Mine," he snarled, nipping her earlobe as he redoubled his efforts before giving one, two, three final strokes, driving deep on the last one as her body arched and she cried out.

Anders' body shuddered as he held himself tight against her, his cock spurting great ropes of his release deep inside her. Gabriella's body convulsed and her pussy contracted, milking his cock for everything he had. He pumped his seed into her, filling her with a torrent of his cum. Her body went through a series of mini orgasms that felt like aftershocks as he collapsed on top of her, allowing her to take his full weight.

They lay there, resplendent in the aftermath. Gabriella stroked his back, purring in his ear and basking in the monumental and reciprocal pleasure he had provided her. He reminded himself that at some point he'd need to get up and lock their chamber door. Anders wanted no possibility of being disturbed until he was finished with her. He meant to take full advantage of all she had to offer. She'd survive the night but would be stiff and sore from his repeated use come morning.

Finally, he rolled away from her. She turned with him, raising herself on her elbow, pushing her red hair out of her face. "You can be such a bastard.

Don't think that any of what just happened means I'm not still pissed at you for not taking me with you. Honestly, I don't know why I don't leave you."

Anders chuckled. He'd heard this all before. "I would remind you, you tried that once before and got your bottom spanked for your trouble. I would think a Rhodes Scholar would not need to be reminded who rules her heart, mind, body, and soul."

Gabriella huffed and curled up against him. "You have no idea how annoying I find all that."

He chuckled again. "I know, my beautiful *villkatt*, but I don't care. How would I live without yours when I have given you mine?"

"I'm pretty sure you got the better end of that deal."

"Of course, I did. After all, I am the Sentinel of Sabu, and I will have what is mine."

He pulled her to him, his cock beginning to regain its former strength. Anders took possession of her mouth as he pushed her onto her back and began to plunder again the treasure he had found all those years ago.

CHAPTER 2

Musée du Louvre
Paris, France
Six Months Before Present Day

Gabriella glanced at herself in the reflection of the storefront window. Not too bad. She'd handed her keys to the valet and brushed the wrinkles from her black silk cocktail dress. She always felt a tad self-conscious when she visited Paris, especially the Louvre. There was a grace and elegance about the Louvre that demanded respect and admiration. Gabriella had both, but she still never quite felt as though she measured up. She raised her chin a fraction. She'd have to work on that. She came from superior stock, after all. Not only was she the younger sister of the high fashion model known simply as Desiree—one name only like Cher or Madonna but not as famous yet—but she was also the great-grand-daughter of Gabriella Lemas, for whom she was named.

Gabriella Lemas the First had been one of the few and the youngest of the female fighters with the Maquis, the notorious guerilla unit of La Résistance. After France's liberation, she had left France as the war bride of Armand Broussard of New Orleans, Louisiana. There they had raised a family, as well as founded a restaurant and hotel empire.

Gabriella had turned her back on her family's expectations, as well as their fame and wealth, and had graduated from Tulane University with a law degree and a double major in art history and archeology. It was while she was attending Oxford as a Rhodes Scholar that she had seen she could make a difference in the world, righting a terrible wrong. Gabriella had begun to research those pieces of art thought lost or destroyed by the Nazis and work to reunite them with the families of those from whom they, and so much more, had been stolen.

"*Mademoiselle* Broussard?" A young, stylish woman, her black hair cut in a chic, stacked bob and dressed in an off the shoulder red gown that fit her to within an inch of her life, approached.

Gabriella looked around the museum and realized she should have taken Desi up on her offer to come to Paris a bit early to raid Desi's closet or go shopping for a new gown for the event. It would have to be the shopping trip because Gabriella was quite sure she would never fit into one of Desi's dresses. Even so, her old standby black silk cocktail dress was still fashionable. It might not be haute couture, but a little black dress never really went out of style—not according to Audrey Hepburn, at any rate. It certainly filled her needs for something acceptable to wear to gala openings, fundraisers, and trips to the opera or theatre. It made the most of her figure and cleavage while hiding her flaws. And besides, it was comfortable. Gabriella couldn't quite suppress her smile—Desi had once informed her that 'comfortable' was not a style.

Gabriella turned and smiled openly. She knew what everyone expected of her. Her family were wealthy patrons and scions of New Orleans and had a summer home on the French Riviera, a nod to her great-grandmother's birthplace. Her sister was a noted fashion model who made her home and very lucrative living here in Paris. The only reason Gabriella was present at this fundraiser was because her sister had insisted she attend. Desiree loved these kinds of events and tried, usually unsuccessfully, to get her younger sister to come up from Nice and attend as her plus one. Desi also had a bad habit of being late for *everything* and the fundraiser was no exception.

"I'm Gabriella Broussard. I'm sure you're looking for my sister, Desiree. She has yet to arrive…"

"No, *Mademoiselle*, it is you whom I seek. My name is Zofia Bendera."

Gabriella's eyes widened; Zofia Bendera was the

name of her great-grandmother's friend. As this Zofia was just about her age, Gabriella surmised that she, too, must be the namesake of the woman her great-grandmother had thought lost to the concentration camps.

"I see you are familiar with my name. I believe we have relatives who knew each other during the war," the young woman said with a smile.

"Yes. My great-grandmother wrote in her diaries about your great-grandmother and despaired, thinking she had died in one of the concentration camps."

"My great-grandmother Zofia was the one your great-grandmother knew; she was captured and tortured by the Nazis before being taken to one of the camps. She met my great-grandfather there and they survived. I was named for her."

"You said you were looking for me?"

"Yes. I understand you work with finding lost artwork stolen by the Nazis. My family lost a beautiful painting by Leon Wyczółkowski. It was taken from the Warsaw Museum and was never recovered. We had hopes in 2012 when they found some twelve hundred pieces with Hildebrand Gurlitt's son, but we were not so fortunate. I was hoping you could help."

"I'd be more than happy to. Do you have any information about it? I mean, after the disappearance?"

"Nothing concrete that I can take to the authorities, but I have heard whispers about it being among the lost works taken to Norway."

"Norway?" That was interesting. Gabriella had heard some vague rumors, as well—nothing she could pin down, but the same information had resurfaced more than once. "I thought most of the pieces disappeared with the Nazis out of the ratlines through Spain and Italy."

Zofia smiled. "You know your history."

Gabriella laughed softly. "It's kind of my business to know. It's hard to be an art historian if you don't."

"Ah, but we both know you are so much more than that. I know you do not seek notoriety, but your name is spoken of with great respect by people who know what you do and the returns you have either negotiated or engineered. I live in Bergen, Norway with my husband. His great-grandfather was one of those who worked the Shetland Bus operation."

Now, this was intriguing. Gabriella asked her, "Will you join me for a drink?"

"But your sister…"

Gabriella looked down at her watch, a diamond-encrusted family heirloom that had belonged to her namesake. "We've got at least half an hour. Desi is never less than an hour late for anything. I was binge watching a show on one of the streaming services and part of the plot revolved around those who'd been members of the Shetland Bus group. It made me curious, and I've been doing some research. I wasn't aware that they smuggled artwork out, either during or after the war. I must say it's all rather fascinating."

"I couldn't agree more. It wasn't just British operatives or citizens who used it along with supplies and munitions, but some SS officers cut off from other escape routes tried to use it to escape. Some were found out and now rest at the bottom of the North Sea, but some made it, and a few hid their treasure before trying to escape."

"Let's go get a drink and mug one of the waiters for one of those hors d'oeuvres platters. We can find a cozy spot to sit, and you can tell me more about your search. I don't know about you, but my feet are killing me."

Zofia glanced down, looking between both of their pairs of shoes. "Mine, too."

As predicted, Desi was late by another forty-five minutes and it took her an additional thirty to locate Zofia and Gabriella, who were quickly becoming friends.

"Gabriella! There you are!" said Desi, tossing her blonde mane back over her shoulder as she breezed over to Gabriella, giving her an air-kiss to each cheek. "And who is your friend?"

"This is Zofia Bendera. We were talking about a painting her family lost in the war," said Gabriella.

"Oh, must you?" said Desi, pouting. "I have the most delicious man I want you to meet. His name is Anders Jensen. He is one of the patrons here and he was very excited when he realized you were my little sister."

"I know Mr. Jensen. He is from Norway. He lives in a stronghold up above Bergen. They call him the Sentinel of Sabu," said Zofia with a tone that said she might know him but wasn't overly fond of the man. Realizing she might have betrayed her own feelings, Zofia continued, "My husband is a policeman. Mr. Jensen is, how do you say it…?"

"A mafia boss?" supplied Gabriella, who had heard the man's name bandied about on the dark web where stolen paintings were bought and sold.

The fact was she knew quite a bit about the reputed leader of the Valhalla Syndicate. He was a collector of Renaissance masters, Viking antiquities, and curiously, pre-Columbian pottery. They'd come against each other a few times, bidding on stolen paintings, but he usually withdrew if he learned she was in competition for the same piece, which surprised her as normally he was relentless in acquiring what he wanted.

"Is he really?" asked Desi, who liked to play dumb when Gabriella knew for a fact she wasn't.

Gabriella turned to her sister. "You want to introduce me to a gangster?" What the hell was Desi up to?

"You don't know that," said Desi, defending herself.

"It may not be something anyone can prove," said

Zofia, "but there are plenty who know. Those who might have been able to prove it seem to have a nasty habit of disappearing."

"Come on, Gabi. I promised him I'd introduce the two of you," whined Desi, playing the bubble-headed model to the hilt.

Gabriella turned to Zofia. "It seems I need to go meet the Godfather. Are you staying in Paris?"

"Just overnight."

"I would really love to talk to you a bit further. Might we have breakfast? Our family has a restaurant here at Le Montmartre Brasserie in the eighteenth arrondissement?"

After thinking for a moment Zofia seemed to make up her mind. "That would be lovely. It would give us a chance to make some arrangements. Shall we say nine?"

"Nine it is. Just ask them for the Broussard family table. I'll see you then."

"I'm looking forward to it."

"Nice to meet you," said Desi, dismissing Zofia. "Come along. I don't want to keep Anders waiting."

When they were out of earshot of Zofia and where no one could really see them, Gabriella pulled free of Desi's grasp and stopped dead in her tracks. "What are you up to?"

"Me? Nothing. Anders said he knew you by reputation and when he learned you were my sister, he asked me to introduce you."

"Are you sleeping with him?"

Desi laughed. "I don't think one gets a lot of sleep when Anders takes you to his bed—at least, that's what his reputation says."

"This just gets better and better. Now you want to introduce me to a playboy gangster. What kind of older sister are you?" Gabriella knew, but she hated to miss the opportunity to tease her.

"Desi," said a deep male voice with a Norwegian accent that sent shivers up and down Gabriella's spine, "what kind of tawdry tales have you been telling about me?"

"Only the truth, Anders, I swear. Anders, this is my little…"

"And by that she means younger," Gabriella teased.

"I can see your reputation does you justice, *mademoiselle*. Be nice to your beautiful sister and come and dance with me. Desiree, will you allow me to steal Gabriella away from you? The string quartet is playing our song."

Gabriella tried extracting her hand with some degree of decorum, but he had a vice-like grip. Finally, in a desperate bid to be free, Gabriella kicked him in the shins, causing him to release her. "First, we don't have a song. Second, I don't like being manhandled. And third, if your goons get any closer to my sister or me, I'll scream so loud that I'll shatter the glass in the pyramid. You don't want to be responsible for destroying a Parisian landmark, do you?"

"Desiree, would you allow Sig to escort you through the buffet and get you a drink? It seems I have offended Gabriella and need to make amends."

Before Gabriella could say anything, one of the larger men of his entourage moved toward Desiree. Gabriella didn't think she could really shatter glass, but she was willing to give it a try. The Sentinel from Sabu was about to see what happened when you messed with a Cajun girl.

Desi stepped forward, putting herself between Gabriella and Anders. "Actually, Anders, my sister isn't the only one who doesn't like being manhandled. She said no, and where we come from, when a lady says no, a gentleman backs the fuck off."

Gabriella smiled. She hadn't been sure, but it seemed as if her sister still had the overly protective instincts of a mama bear.

"My apologies. Please, Gabriella, they are playing a lovely Bach concerto. I would very much like to dance with you."

"Fine, but my sister stays where she and I can see each other at all times and your goons, as Desi said, back the fuck off."

"As you wish," he said, waving off his men, and offering Gabriella his hand. "Will you allow Sig at least to get your sister a plate and something to drink?"

"Actually, that would be nice. I haven't eaten all day. I'm going to sit over there with the other patrons. If you don't want to go with him…"

Gabriella shot her sister a quick smile. "He's just taking me onto the dance floor, not out into a back alley to put a bullet through my head." At his feigned look of hurt, Gabriella smiled sweetly and said, "your reputation precedes you, as well."

She'd been worried the night would be an endless bore and it had turned out to be anything but. Anders was an exceptional dancer who made even her meager attempts to partner with him look graceful and she found herself relaxing and enjoying the strength and passion she could sense simmering beneath the surface.

As he whirled her around the dance floor, Gabriella wondered what the hell she'd gotten herself into.

CHAPTER 3

Gabriella followed Jensen's lead as if she'd been born ballroom dancing. She almost wished she had taken the time and care to buy a long gown; it would have swept around and added to her façade. Besides, floor length would have allowed her to wear shorter heels and cover up her lousy footwork.

It didn't matter, though; Jensen was good enough to make them both look elegant and graceful. She had no doubt who was leading. He had a firm grip on her hand and the hand at the small of her back kept her close but not inappropriately so. She was, however, close enough that she could inhale his scent. It wasn't overpowering and seemed almost as if it came from the man himself—strong, clean, hypnotic. Gabriella had to remind herself that the man she was enjoying dancing with was a gangster. And yet, she had to admit she was intrigued as to why he wanted to dance with her.

"You had your way, Mr. Jensen. Now, what is it you want?" asked Gabriella as they glided smoothly through the other couples on the dance floor amidst priceless works of art.

"As I said, a chance to meet with you and perhaps an opportunity to sit down and discuss a business matter I think you might be interested in."

"I don't normally do business with gangsters."

"You wound me," he said dramatically. "And I know for a fact you have done business with those with far less savory reputations than mine. We may be able to help one another locate certain masterpieces that have gone missing."

"If you know the whereabouts of stolen paintings, you are obligated to inform the authorities."

"But, as you say, I am a gangster and my information, as well as where and how I obtained it, might not withstand the scrutiny of some of those authorities. I am willing to pay you a finder's fee, as well as allow you to reunite all but one of the paintings with the surviving members of the families from whom they were stolen."

"But you'll keep one for yourself. If you know where they are, why not go in guns blazing and simply take what you want?"

"I am not willing to risk the destruction of the paintings." He twirled them to a stop in the middle of the dance floor. Gabriella was surprised when people simply danced around them. "At least meet with me."

Gabriella removed her hand and stepped back. "No, Mr. Jensen, I don't think I will." She turned away and went to join her sister, who was sitting with the Parisian equivalent of the police commissioner. Anders nodded his head and smiled before removing himself from the dance floor.

Anders watched her walk away. He probably shouldn't have enlisted her sister's aid in meeting her, but the temptation to do so had been too hard to resist. They had crossed paths more than once, more than she even knew. She was a relentless pursuer of stolen art and antiquities, most often working for individuals who could only afford her because of the finder's fees often attached. Although, he was also aware of the many cases she had taken *pro bono*.

The feminine sway to her backside held his interest and was alluring to say the least. He couldn't help but admire her gorgeous ass and it looked to be firm, round, and very spankable. He wondered if any man had ever held her accountable and subjected her to his discipline when she acted out. He had no doubt whatsoever that Gabriella would act out. He allowed his gaze to take in the rest of her retreating figure— tall and far more curvaceous than her willowy sister.

He had not expected to see Zofia Bendera here in Paris. She lived in Bergen with her husband, who was a police officer. He had no idea of Anders' true nature, but he knew that Anders was of a different ilk than most mafia bosses and tended to work more often with the police than against them. He would need to find out why Zofia was here and what she wanted with Gabriella Broussard.

Desiree Broussard had taken up a strategic place from which to keep an eye on her sister. She could easily see them on the dance floor and was sitting next to Paris' chief of police. Anders and the gentleman were acquainted but did not enjoy the friendliest of relationships. Normally, it was not an issue as Anders kept most of his dealings to Scandinavia, with an occasional foray into Germany or Russia.

Ah, there was the rub. The Russian mob, known as the bratva, were a bunch of notorious thugs and killers. Their rivalries and wars with each other were the stuff of legend. They were undisciplined, unruly, and seemed to revel in violence for violence's sake. They were becoming a problem. Joshua Knight of England had asked for the help of the Northern Lights Coalition and Anders, Lars, and Gunnar had agreed when they met that it was in their best interest to join forces with Knight and his cohorts. They had forged a mutual pact of protection and if the damn Cosa Nostra could be persuaded to join them, they'd have the bratva nicely contained.

Even if he and Lars hadn't agreed that it made sense to try and limit the bratva's growing presence, Gunnar would have had no choice. His mate was Knight's younger sister. When the bratva had tried to strike at Hammerfall, they found that Gunnar had married a woman of rare quality. It was said that she had acted as his beta and been instrumental in defeating the attack. Anders smiled. He rather imagined Gabriella would be of a similar ferocity.

He looked up and found Gabriella looking at him. She glanced away, but he had seen curiosity and something more in her gaze. He would find a way to persuade her to meet with him. She was vital to his quest to obtain Albrecht Durer's A Lying Lioness, a small drawing done somewhere between 1471 and 1528.

It had been stolen by an SS Officer named Mühlmann, who many believed to be the greatest art thief who ever lived. He was captured in the Austrian Alps and although he testified against many higher-ranking Nazi officials, he was taken to Munich by the Americans, where he managed to escape in 1948. He was said to have lived in Bavaria, but part of the information Anders had obtained had placed him at various locations in Norway, including Bergen and its surrounding fjords.

Anders nodded to his men, who surreptitiously left the festivities and joined him at the main entrance with the SUV.

"Are we headed to the Four Seasons, Anders?" said his driver.

"You are. I am not," replied Anders. "I will be staying at the Broussard's boutique hotel. That should afford me a way to cross paths again with the alluring Gabriella."

"She seemed fairly immune to your charms," quipped Sig, who was the head of Anders' security team and an old and trusted friend.

"I have not yet begun to court my mate. Mark my words, old friend, the beautiful Gabriella will be mine."

Sig grinned. "Of that I have no doubt. There will be many females, both shifter and not, who will be sorry to hear the Sentinel of Sabu is no longer available." He turned to the rest of their men. "That will leave more for the rest of us."

"Take yourselves to the hotel or to one of the clubs, gentlemen. Have fun. But not too much. And you be careful. Paris is not a safe city. The bratva are strong here and you are now someone they consider a sworn enemy."

"The day I can't handle a bunch of bratva thugs is the day you should start looking for a new Sentinel. Go on, I will be fine. You forget I spent my college days here in Paris." He smiled, mostly to himself.

"Did you actually study anything other than the fine Parisian ladies?"

"I knew where my destiny lay and knew my father

didn't have long to live so I decided to do something that pleased me. I studied and graduated from Le Cordon Bleu here in Paris. My father had trained me in our business, and it amused me to learn to cook. Now, it would seem my fated mate comes from a long-line of business-minded chefs. I should fit right in." He began to walk away from them, waving his hand over his head without looking back.

Given the sound and mood of his men, Anders was fairly sure they would not be headed for the hotel straight away. There was a time he would have joined them and unleashed his legendary sexual appetite, but those days were done, and he was surprised at how glad he was of it. Now he wanted one woman and one only—Gabriella Broussard. He wondered idly if she even knew of the existence of shifters.

The clouds grew thick, and the sky overhead began to indulge in its favorite Paris drizzle. Anders turned his collar up to ward off the cold and decided to take the most direct route, cutting through the back streets and alleys. He was within the last mile of the Broussard hotel when he could feel the presence of humans, some following and some running—he assumed to cut him off. He almost felt sorry for them; they were in for a fight they weren't expecting.

He saw the three men who had thought to box him in ahead. Two had followed from behind to ensure he continued the way they wanted. When Anders was practically at the midsection between them, he stopped, removing his cashmere overcoat and hanging it off the railing of a fire escape to keep it from getting dirty. He toed off his formal shoes and removed his tuxedo, rendering him naked.

"Woo hoo! A strip show," called one of those who would most likely not live to see the sunrise.

"We're not wired that way," called another.

And a third one, "I don't know, I go both ways and the man's got a nice ass."

"Give us your valuables," said one who had a short baton in his fist that he thumped against the outstretched palm of his other hand. "And let Claude have your ass and we'll let you live."

Anders smiled. Parisian street accents. They weren't bratva. That was good. He wouldn't need to worry about retaliation. If any of them managed to get away, no one would ever believe what was about to happen. Anders lifted his face to the sky, allowing the rain to fall down and invigorate him. He craned his neck in a circle as he called forth his great beast.

A cloud of silver, laced with the colors of the aurora borealis, began to shimmer and envelop him. He could feel the warmth of the change as it overtook him and the enormous snow leopard that lived within came rushing to the fore. His body shifted from man to beast as the snow leopard took his place in the Parisian alley.

He could sense the fear of all five men and hear the urine trickling down the leg of one of those behind him. Their sense of dread and panic was the greatest and they would be slower to move. Best to take out those to the front.

Whirling around, Anders leapt toward the leader of the group, grabbing his jugular vein and ripping it open as he slashed at his midsection, disemboweling and leaving him dead before he ever turned loose. The two who had stood with him started forward, reconsidered, and turned to run. They didn't make it. He grabbed the head of one in his powerful jaws, shaking him and snapping his neck in one motion, while he used his back feet to rip open the other man's guts, leaving him to try and grab at them to keep them from falling on the ground.

Anders turned towards his two lesser opponents, one of whom was trying to bring a gun to bear on the beast who charged down the alley. It didn't work. Anders grabbed the wrist of the hand that held the gun and tore it off. Blood spurted everywhere as the man tried to scream but was cut off as Anders ripped open his throat, rendering him speechless and dead.

The last of his would-be assailants dropped to his knees. He was barely an adult. Anders didn't think he'd even left his teens.

"Please don't kill me. Please," the boy begged.

Anders bade his snow leopard to retreat. He stood, the blood from his attackers dripping from what had been his claws. "Why should I let you live? We both know your leader would have shown me no mercy even if I had given him everything he asked for."

"I know. I know," the youth said, panicking. "If you let me live, I'll leave Paris forever. No one here will ever see me again. I'll be gone before sunrise. Please. Please. I'll go back to my father's farm and make him proud. Please."

"Your name?"

"Lucas Touchard. My family called me Luc."

"What brought you to Paris?" Anders said, grabbing the young man's collar and dragging him back to where he'd left his clothes.

"I thought I wanted excitement. You know, big city, bright lights. But I hate it here. I know you have no reason to believe me, but I swear I've been trying to squirrel enough away to buy a train ticket home."

Anders looked at the boy who was so obviously out of place. Once he was dressed, he took out his wallet and handed him two hundred euros. "Do not go back to wherever you were staying. You leave here and go to the train station. Buy a ticket home and when you get there, you buy your mother something nice and beg your parents' forgiveness."

"I will do what you say, but if I buy a second-class train ticket and some flowers for my mother, I will have quite a bit left over to give to my father to help out."

Anders nodded and peeled off another three

hundred euros; the boy's eyes widened in disbelief. "Do not make me regret my generosity or mercy."

"No, sir. You won't. I swear it. I will never tell another soul about what I saw."

Anders chuckled. "Who would believe you? Now go and do something with your life."

"I will, monsieur. If you ever need help in Nice, my parents have a small dairy farm. Send someone for me and I will do whatever you ask." The boy finally got to his feet. "I will find a way to repay my debt to you one day."

"Live a good life. Be happy, don't rob people, and I will mark your debt as paid."

The young man turned and ran as Anders pulled his cashmere coat on, turned the collar back up and then began to make his way to the Broussard's hotel. He chuckled to himself. He had made contact with the woman he believed could help him find the Durer's Lioness, he had kept a young man from making a mess of his life, and he had found his fated mate. All in all, not a bad evening.

CHAPTER 4

He entered the beautiful boutique hotel the Broussards had built in Montmartre. It was elegant without being pretentious. Old world without being moldy. He hoped they had a room for him.

"*Comment puis-je vous aider, monsieur?*" said the front desk clerk.

"Any chance you speak English or Norwegian?" asked Anders. "I'm afraid my secondary school French and what I remember from my time at Le Cordon Bleu is atrocious."

"But, of course, sir. How may I help you?"

"Thank God."

The young man chuckled. "Are you looking for a room?"

"I am, indeed. The best you have."

"We have one room left. It's not a suite. There's

an event at the Louvre and one of the family is visiting Paris."

Anders could feel her presence even before he could detect her scent.

"I have yet to unpack, Guy. I'll take the smaller room. Have someone go up and get my bag and move it down. Give Mr. Jensen our finest and see that he is extended every courtesy we have to offer," said Gabriella. "Are you following me, Mr. Jensen?"

"Anders, please. I didn't follow you, per se, but I must admit after you left me so pitifully alone on the dance floor, I decided to forego my usual suite at the Four Seasons and see if I could get a room here."

"And what would you have done if we were full, or I refused your business?"

"I didn't think you could be so cruel twice in one evening and I felt it was worth the risk to be able to have a chance encounter with you."

Gabriella laughed and Anders smiled. She had a laugh that was wondrous and full of life.

"Mr. Jensen, as we say in New Orleans, you are so full of shit, your eyes are turning brown."

"You are being so kind; might I press my luck and get you to let me buy you a drink?"

"The bar is closing, and before you ask, I have a breakfast meeting."

"Surely one of the owners of the hotel can get them to sell me a bottle of wine and then join me in my suite for a glass or two."

Shaking her head, Gabriella asked, "Red or white?"

"A bottle of the finest of your preference."

"Guy, ask them to send up a bottle of Prieur Montrachet along with a fruit and cheese plate." She turned to Anders, "I'm hungry. I never did have a chance to eat anything."

"Well, we can't have that. Show me to the kitchen and I'll make us a real meal, and then I'll clean up afterward."

"I don't know, monsieur," started Guy. "Chef is very particular."

"I got my degree from Le Cordon Bleu. I promise, I won't make a mess."

Gabriella smiled. "Tell Chef I was hungry, and Mr. Jensen offered to cook for me. This way," she said, leading him back to the kitchen.

Anders made himself at home, rolling up the sleeves to his tuxedo shirt, revealing forearms rippled with muscle. If the hotel's chef thought this kitchen was well appointed, he'd kill to cook at the Sabu Stronghold. Granted, his kitchen probably fed more people than the hotel on a daily basis.

"Scallops," he said, opening the refrigerator. "Do you like them?"

"I was born and raised in New Orleans. I grew up eating seafood, but scallops are probably my favorite shellfish."

He turned around. "Even more than lobster?"

"Absolutely."

"Good; me, too."

Anders assembled the ingredients he needed for Coquilles St. Jacques as well as garlic rosemary polenta.

"I feel fairly decadent sitting here doing nothing except letting you cook for me. Can I do anything to help?"

"Can you stir the polenta? It needs to be..."

"Stirred continually. Raised in a family of chefs and hoteliers."

Anders smiled as she stepped up to the saucepan and began to stir the polenta. He came up behind her, slipped an apron over her head, and tied it around her waist, holding her a bit closer and a bit longer than was absolutely necessary and praying she couldn't feel how hard his cock was.

When the polenta was ready, Gabriella said, "I'll go get the wine. Let's eat in here. It'll be easier."

He took a moment and indulged himself in watching her walk away. The woman had a sinner's figure and a truly glorious ass. He wanted desperately to see her naked, splayed out on their bed and ready for his claiming. She was going to make a spectacular mistress to the clan.

By the time she returned, he'd found a handful of small tealights which he arranged on a non-flammable serving platter and had set their food out at the chef's table—he at the head and her to the right.

"Wow, I'm impressed. I have to tell you; I had a taste of your polenta. I want the recipe."

"I tell you what. I will trade you the recipe for a half an hour of your time tomorrow to listen to my business proposal."

"Done."

They settled down and Anders watched as she tried the Coquilles St. Jacques that he had prepared as a main dish, served alongside the polenta that she had helped make. She put her first fork full of the scallops in her mouth. Gabriella closed her eyes, smiled, and moaned with pleasure. He'd forgotten how much he liked cooking for people. Perhaps they would carve out two date nights each week—one in which they went into Bergen or anywhere she wanted and the other where they declared the kitchen off limits, and he cooked for her.

"Divine," she said. "Seriously. I've had this dish a thousand times and this is the best. If I give you a full hour of my time, can I have your recipe for the scallops as well?"

Anders laughed. "To see you enjoy my food, how can I deny you? Both are yours with nothing due from you in return."

"I thought you were supposed to be a shrewd businessman."

"No. You think I am a gangster."

"I know you are. The police chief confirmed that, but then added that you were an honorable one—

never touching drugs of any kind. But how do you feel about prostitution?"

"In Norway the selling of sexual services is perfectly legal, but the purchase of them is not."

Gabriella started to laugh. "You can't be serious!"

Anders held up his hand. "On my honor, I swear it is true."

Her mobile rang and Gabriella glanced at the caller ID, frowning and picking up the call. "Desi? What's wrong?"

He couldn't hear Desi's answer, but the way Gabriella's body began to tremble told him it wasn't good. He grabbed his own phone and texted his driver:

Bring the SUV now!

"No. If you're sure no one else is there, lock the door and stay put. I'll come to you. We can figure out what you want to do from there." She ended the call. "I'm sorry. I have to go. Desi was attacked in her flat."

"My SUV is enroute from the Four Seasons. We'll take you to Desi and make sure you're both safe. I'll leave someone behind to clean up."

"Not necessary. I'll get someone to do it. I think I'd like to have you with me."

Taking her chin in his hand. "Whatever has happened, I will ensure everything is handled in whatever way you want, and that you and Desi are safe. Do you have security here at the hotel?"

"Yes."

"Good. Let's go coordinate with them and Guy."

Anders led her out to the front desk, wrapping his arm around her waist.

"Guy, call security. Get someone to clean up the kitchen and move Gabriella's bag back up to the better suite. Does it have two or more beds?"

"Oui, monsieur."

"Good. Desi will be returning with us."

"Someone called for security?" said a beefy guard with a military haircut and bearing.

"Yes, if you're the only one here, you need to call your people in. Gabriella's sister has been attacked. We're going to get her, but I want to ensure the hotel is secure."

"I'll see to it," said the guard.

The SUV screeched to a stop outside the hotel's entrance. Anders grasped Gabriella's elbow and steered her out. The back door to the SUV was open and his men were between the entrance and the vehicle, guns drawn. He steered her into the SUV, and they flew down the streets of Paris, arriving at Desiree's flat in record time.

Once again, Anders' men got out of the SUV and ensured the street was safe before opening the door into the building. Anders whisked her inside, taking the vintage elevator to the top floor. The doors to the elevator opened and Anders held her back as his men checked the foyer. The top floor only had three flats.

"I don't know what we're walking into, but thank

you," said Gabriella as she knocked on her sister's door. "Desi? Desi? It's Gabi. Open the door."

The door cracked open, "Who are those men with guns?" Desi asked, trying to close the door.

"It's okay, Desi. They work for Anders. He was at the hotel when you called. Can you let us in?"

Desi admitted Gabriella, Anders, and one of his men. The other two closed the door behind them and took up flanking positions in the foyer.

Anders looked around the flat. Someone had trashed it. "Desi, are you all right?"

She nodded, her fingers twitching against the fabric of her dress as Gabriella led her to the settee and sat down with her. "What happened?"

"I stayed a little longer than you and the Louvre's head of security gave me a lift home. He dropped me off and I came upstairs. When I started to open my door, I got jerked inside. They had already trashed my place. They slapped me around and were shouting at me in what I think was Russian."

Anders growled and both women looked at him. "Bratva."

"The Russian mob? What the fuck do they want with my sister?"

"Unknown. Desi, have you ever crossed them? Worked for a designer who did?"

"No. I swear. I…" Desi started shivering.

"It can wait," said Anders. "Let's get you back to the hotel. I'll call the police and have one of my people meet them in the morning. They can do whatever French police do in this situation and then I'll have the place put back in order."

"I can take care of my sister," said Gabriella a bit defensively. Anders drew in a breath for patience. She might as well start learning now that she could turn to him and trust that he would take care of things.

"Yes. You take care of Desi and allow me to handle the rest. Come on, ladies, let's get you home."

Once everyone was safely back at the family's hotel and up in the suite, Anders left one of his men inside and went to speak to Sig. "You get hold of our man in the police department. See that he takes a personal interest. Call Sabu and tell them we'll be here for a while. Have a group of our men come to relieve you."

"I will stay with you."

"No. I don't like leaving our people for any length of time without you, me or Nils being there. I want to know if it was bratva and which family. If those bastards were looking to pick a fight, they came to the right man."

"Anders…"

"Sig, I won't leave her. I'll try to get them to agree to come to Sabu."

"What if they don't agree?" asked Sig.

"They will," responded Anders with a grin. "I can be very persuasive. Tell Dagmar to have rooms prepared for them."

Sig nodded. "I understand. I don't like it, but I understand. I would prefer if you stayed in the room with them. I don't have enough men with me to cover two rooms."

"There's no way in hell I'm going anywhere else tonight. Do you have your spare gun?"

"I do," said Sig, leaning down to get his Glock and handing it to Anders. "We've got you covered, and our people will be here by morning. I want to bring a larger security force."

"No, just four will do. I don't want to spook the girls. But get the police on it and I want answers by morning."

"I'll see to it."

Anders let himself back in, and the man who'd been inside took up position just outside the door. He wanted answers and he wanted them now. Were this Norway, not only would people be jumping to help him, but they would also be asking how high he wanted them to jump.

Damn, he hated France sometimes.

CHAPTER 5

Gabriella woke to the smell of bacon. It had to be the perfect scent to wake up to. No, that wasn't right. The perfect scent would be a naked Anders Jensen warm up against her body… and bacon. No, that wasn't right either. She was *not* attracted to Anders Jensen. *Liar!* screamed her libido. *Shut up!* responded her brain.

She rolled over, grabbing her phone just before the alarm went off. Ugh! She had to get showered and get downstairs to meet with Zofia. But first, bacon.

She rolled off the bed and padded to the double doors of her suite. Desi had opted for the other bedroom. She opened the door and the first thing she saw was the way the sunlight streamed through the doors from the balcony as if God himself had done the lighting for her sister. She looked gorgeous.

Gabriella didn't even want to think about how she looked.

"Anders, it was just so kind of you to come last night. I'm so glad Gabi was with you. I didn't think the two of you had hit it off at the fundraiser," said Desi.

"Your sister was only able to resist my charm for so long," replied Anders, taking a sip of his coffee and looking as though he was hanging on Desi's every word.

Why shouldn't he? Desi had been wrapping men around her finger since before Gabriella was even born.

"Gabi! God, you look like shit," exclaimed Desi.

"Morning, Desi, good to see you, too," mumbled Gabriella, reaching to take a piece of bacon from a plate on the trolley which held numerous serving dishes piled high with food.

"Desiree, shame on you, your sister looks beautiful," said Anders. "Good morning, Gabriella, sit down and I'll fix you a plate."

Gabriella arched an eyebrow at him. "Bullshit." Deciding that this morning was already starting off badly, she took the entire plate of bacon. "Fuck it," she muttered, wandering toward the window and deciding it was entirely too bright outside.

"You'll have to forgive Gabi. She doesn't always wake up well," Desi said, apologizing for her as

Gabriella retreated to her bedroom and closed the door behind her.

Gabriella wondered if Desi realized how many times she apologized for or explained her little sister. It was really annoying. Gabriella knew she would never measure up to her beautiful, talented, gracious, and unfailingly polite older sister. Well, that wasn't true. Desi was only polite right up until someone threatened her or someone she loved. Then she had all the charm of a rabid junkyard dog.

Gabriella smiled. For all her faults, and there really weren't that many, Gabriella adored her older sister. They were nothing at all alike. Desi was the perfect daughter for a family of their social standing in New Orleans. Which wasn't to imply that Gabriella had no outstanding traits. She did, as well. Unfortunately, according to their mother, they were more suited to a boy. The more her mother had tried to make Gabriella conform to the societal norm for a well-bred young lady, the more Gabriella had rebelled.

She managed to eat three pieces of bacon and use the Keurig that was located on the nightstand and make a cup of coffee. By the time she'd pulled her long red curls up into a high ponytail and adjusted the shower temperature, she'd finished her first cup of coffee, started her second and scarfed up all the bacon. Taking the mug into the shower with her, she held it so that none of the hot water that was cascading down around her diluted her strong French roast.

Once she was clean and had washed the sleep from her eyes and body, she stepped out of the shower, placing her empty mug on the countertop as she dried off. Gabriella smiled. It had not escaped her notice that her sister had appeared to greet the morning in full make-up and beautifully coiffed hair. Deciding her hair was fine as it was for the day's activities, she applied tinted moisturizer to her face, a little color to her cheeks, eyeliner and mascara. She pulled on her favorite soft wool and silk blend sweater and a pair of faded jeans, which she tucked into a pair of cowboy boots. Ready to face the world, she flung open the door to re-enter the hotel room's sitting area.

"I hope now that you've eaten all the bacon and had at least one cup of coffee," started Desi who smiled as Gabriella held up two fingers, "I stand corrected, two cups of coffee. I hope you can find it in your miserable little soul to be pleasant."

Gabriella hid a smile as she recognized the narrowing of Anders' eyes, just for a moment, at the perceived insult from Desi. That wasn't normal. Most men doted on Desi and made every excuse in the world for some of her more outrageous behaviors, but she didn't deserve to have a man like Anders Jensen thinking ill of her.

"You'll have to forgive Desi," said Gabriella. "I

think she's forgotten that we just met last night. Do you have a sister?"

"Unfortunately, I was an only child."

"Well, I'm not sure if that was unfortunate or not," said Gabriella.

"Bitch," laughed Desi.

"Takes one to know one," responded Gabriella in the same way she had since they were children before looking at Anders.

It was hard to look at Anders Jensen, at least hard to look and not drool. The man was gorgeous, and she rather imagined he was catnip to all of the women she was sure fluttered around him like the proverbial moth to a flame. He was tall, well over six feet, broad shouldered, lean waisted and judging by the forearms she had seen when he'd rolled up his sleeves, with an exceedingly muscular physique and a face that was beautifully angular in its symmetry. Some men were just brutally handsome, and Gabriella thought the description was appropriate for Anders.

Gabriella smiled as he tugged his ear in confusion.

"The problem with not having a sibling, especially an older one, is that you don't understand the dynamics involved. Desi and I can say the worst things to each other and have occasionally indulged in an outright cat fight. But if anyone, and I do mean anyone, tries to come between us..."

"—we band together to beat the shit out of

them," finished Desi. "In our relationship, 'bitch' is a term of endearment."

Anders shook his head, the corners of his mouth lifting into an easy and devastating smile. "Then I should not admonish Desiree when she is mean to you."

"No," said Gabriella, grinning. "Feel free. God knows, nobody else does."

Desi's light, bubbly laughter filled the room like champagne trickling down one of those silly fountains that were so popular at weddings. "Like I said," Desi drawled, "bitch. And bitch, did you eat all the bacon?"

"I did and it was delicious," said Gabriella, leaning in her sister's direction and sticking out her tongue.

"You are a truly vile creature. See Anders? At least you didn't have to suffer as I have."

Anders' chuckle was deep, melodic, and felt a great deal like warm salted caramel sauce drizzling over soft-serve vanilla ice cream. Gabriella was not overly fond of chocolate, but if that man wanted to cover his body in hot fudge, she'd be the first one to sign up to lick it off. She needed to leave and now. The last thing she wanted was to develop a crush on a gangster.

Gabriella turned to head out for her meeting with Zofia. She hadn't made it very far before Anders placed his body as a kind of barricade between her and the door. She hadn't seen or heard him move. Last night it had occurred to her that he moved with a predatory grace most often reserved for large cats—tigers, lions, leopards, and the like.

"Excuse me?" she said, taking a step back.

"Where are you going?" he said, staring her down in what could be construed as a very intimidating way.

"I'm tempted to say none of your damn business," she shot back. Taking a deep breath and expelling it slowly, she continued, "I have a meeting downstairs with a potential client."

"Who?"

"That information is confidential."

"Zofia Bendera?"

"As I said, that information is confidential."

"Is she trying to recover Wyczółkowski's Bust of a Young Woman?"

"What problem are you having with the concept of confidentiality?"

Gabriella could tell she was getting to him. She wondered how many people dared to argue with a man of his wealth and power—not many, she'd guess. Gabriella watched as he seemed to force the tension from his neck and shoulders, relaxing what had become a rigid posture.

"The business matter I wanted to discuss with you involves those who took the Wyczółkowski painting, as well as a drawing I wish to acquire."

"You expect me to help you 'acquire'—nice choice of words—a drawing, presumably worth a fortune, looted by the Nazis?" Anders said nothing. "You do know part of what I do is track down guys like you and either 'acquire' the item for the rightful owner or see the bad guys put behind bars, right? I'm willing to make allowances because you were of immeasurable assistance last night…"

"And she thinks you're hot," called Desi from the settee, watching her confrontation with Anders as if it were a preview of coming attractions in the theatre. All she needed was a tub of buttery popcorn, an overpriced soda and some bubblegum sticking to the underside of her seat.

Gabriella glanced over her shoulder. "You are such a pain in the ass."

"Rumor has it, Mr. Jensen could take care of that for you." Desi was clearly enjoying herself.

"My sister's erroneous assumptions aside," she glanced down at her heirloom watch, "I have an appointment at nine."

"Your meeting must be close by or else you'll be late."

"As you seem so concerned, I will tell you my meeting is downstairs in the restaurant."

"Good. I will have one of my men keep your sister company and I will accompany you."

Gabriella could feel her rein on her infamous temper loosening. She had to consciously think about not stomping her foot like a five-year-old. She focused on controlling her voice and tone as she said, "You really do have a problem with the concept of confidentiality, don't you?"

"Not at all," he said, the set of his shoulders squaring, locking into place, showing that he believed he had command of the situation. "I swore last night to keep you and your sister safe, and I will do that."

"Not that I don't appreciate what you did, but there's no way to know what happened at Desi's wasn't some isolated, random incident."

"I believe we both know better. Those men were bratva."

"Not every thug with a Russian accent is a member of the Russian mafia. And given your reputation, I think you'd be a bit more careful about slinging accusations."

"The Valhalla Syndicate is *nothing* like the bratva. Nothing. If they believe your sister has something they want, they won't stop until they get it."

"I didn't know there was some kind of hierarchy among goon squads. Now, please," she said, trying to push past him but failing to do so, "I am going to my meeting."

"I will either accompany you or you will not go. I am willing to compromise and sit where I can keep you in sight at all times, but not overhear you."

"You do realize that I have no need to compromise with you and this is my family's hotel, and I can always have our security..."

"Your security men will not move against me or those who answer to me."

"You're an arrogant sonofabitch, I'll give you that. Even if you can intimidate our staff, I can call the police."

"I fear you will find they have no interest in crossing me," he said calmly, provoking a giggle from Desi.

She whipped her head around to look at Desi, who was totally entranced by her and Anders' interaction. "You could do something to help."

"Okay," said Desi. "Be careful, Anders; she has a reputation for kneeing guys in the balls and I've heard yours would make a sizeable target."

Gabriella stared open-mouthed while Anders laughed. "You're no help at all."

"Thank you for that insight into your sister's character."

"What insight could you possibly get from that bullshit remark?" said Gabriella, exasperated.

"That you fight to win and aren't afraid to fight dirty to do so."

"He's got you there," laughed Desi.

"I am so putting coconut into something you eat or drink," retorted Gabriella.

Anders furrowed his brow. "Why coconut? Does she not like it?"

"Just the opposite. She absolutely adores it, but it gives her hives for at least forty-eight hours."

"As I said, you fight dirty."

"I fight," Gabriella said, taking a step into his personal space, "to win."

"Well said, my little *villkatt*," he chuckled without taking a step back.

"What the hell is a *villkatt*?" asked Gabriella, shaking her head.

"It is Norwegian for wildcat," Anders responded. "To be fair, you should know two things. If you ever knee or kick me in the groin, I have an exceptionally fast recovery and I will have you face down over my knee so quickly it will make your head spin. The second is that I know how to make a *villkatt* purr."

Gabriella rolled her eyes as two thoughts flitted across her brain independent of one another. The first was that he was an arrogant jerk and the second was being grateful that he had no way of knowing how much the idea of his doing just that and using her roughly afterwards turned her on. There wasn't any way he could know that, right?

The gleam in his eye made her wonder and unsettled her just the faintest amount.

CHAPTER 6

*A*nders stepped out of her way, gesturing to the door, "We are agreed?"

Gabriella glanced at her watch again. She hated being late. She thought it was rude and unprofessional, unless, of course, you were Desi. Then it was adorable and expected.

"Fine, but I intend to tell the person I'm meeting with who you are, that you have a proposal you think might benefit her and point you out *across the room*."

"You see? We are in complete agreement," he said, opening the door to usher her through and motioning to one of his men. "Ask Nils to come to the hotel. I want him to stay inside the room and keep Desiree company."

The man nodded and stepped a discreet distance away before turning back. "He was on his way and is coming up now."

"Excellent," said Anders, brightening considerably when a good-looking hunk stepped out of the elevator and headed to their room. I need you to stay inside with Desiree." He caught Gabriella by the arm to prevent her rushing away from him and after introducing the two sisters to Nils, said to Desi, "You behave yourself. When your sister and I return, we shall have lunch and I should have some information to share with you."

He closed the door and waited to hear the lock click into place before leading Gabriella to the elevator. Once inside, he pushed the button for the lobby.

"Shouldn't you tell your men we're on the move? It's what they do in the movies."

"Which is only one of the things the movies get wrong in this kind of scenario. Trust me, the man I left at the door of your room has already called to tell them. They'll be waiting when the elevator doors open."

And they were.

"This is ridiculous," she seethed as he took her elbow and guided her to the restaurant. There was no way for her to dislodge his hand without making a scene.

"This is how it will be," he said smoothly in a way that made her feel like he was purring to her, the sound seeping through the pores of her skin and taking up residence in the marrow of her bones. He chuckled. "So, your potential new client is in fact

Zofia Bendera. Before you reject her case, do both her and me a favor and hear me out."

"I told you, I don't deal with thugs."

"Gabriella, you must quit referring to me as a thug. Syndicate master, mafia don, or alpha to my clan. Or, the people of Bergen, as well as others, call me the Sentinel of Sabu."

"Sabu isn't a very Norwegian-sounding word."

"It isn't. It is what those in the Himalayas call the snow leopard."

"Snow leopard? They're very rare, aren't they?"

"You know your large cats."

Anders took her hand in his, brought it to his lips and kissed the back of it. The feel of his lips was like soft pillows of velvet. It should be illegal for a man to have lips that felt like that. She wondered what they might feel like wrapped around one of her nipples or her clit. When the hell had she started fantasizing about having a liaison with some gangster? *Not just any gangster*, her mind whispered, *Anders Jensen*.

"I'll be over there. If you need me, just nod your head in my direction," he said, still holding her hand close to those incredible lips and looking deep into her eyes.

Gabriella had to think about breathing as she said, "I don't know why I feel inclined to say thank you…"

"Because your parents taught you well, and you recognize your Master when you meet him."

Gabriella closed her hand into a fist and tried to

punch him in the mouth but couldn't move her hand forward to make contact. The laughter in his eyes was not in the least derisive. He had more strength and they both knew it.

Before she could say or do anything, Anders turned her towards the table and patted her backside. *What the hell had he meant by that?* She knew what she thought he meant, or rather what her secret fantasy hoped he meant. He couldn't possibly know about the club in Dante's where she and Desi indulged in their desire for D/s sex. Neither of them could live the lifestyle, but both enjoyed the ability to lose themselves in a submissive role and give over to a well-trained Dom.

Zofia smiled as Gabriella reached the table. "I hadn't expected to see you with Anders Jensen."

"Do you know him?"

Zofia laughed. "No. We don't travel in the same social circles, but I don't think there is anyone in Norway who doesn't know the Sentinel of Sabu."

"That's an odd moniker." Seeing confusion, Gabriella clarified. "Nickname."

"Ah, yes. His people have held the land around Bergen for as long as such things have been recorded and as the Sabu Stronghold has stood. Anders is the leader of the clan and extends his protection to Bergen as well as the surrounding area. But still, you can understand my curiosity."

"Yes, and I'm not *with* him. He is staying in the hotel. My sister's apartment was ransacked, and she was roughed up, although thank God, nothing serious. Anders was here at the hotel when it happened, and he helped me go and get Desi. He's been very gracious but is now being an overbearing asshole."

"*Yah*, but a very handsome and sexy overbearing asshole." Zofia's eyes were shining with humor.

"Very. But that's not what you're here for. Tell me about the painting."

She pulled a large legal folder, complete with dividers and annotated tabs. When she caught Gabriella's stare, she smiled. "I work for lawyers."

"Then forgive me, but why not ask them?"

"I did. They said it would be far too expensive for them to help *pro bono* and my husband and I do not have the funds. One of the senior partners told me about you and that you would take a finder's fee, but I don't have that kind of money."

"Let's see if I think I can help you and then figure out how to pay for it. It may not be as expensive as you think, and I may have another way to cover the cost."

"My great-grandmother and her family were caught up in the madness that was the Nazi regime in Poland. More than half her family were hauled off in the middle of the night, along with all their valuables. Paintings, sculptures, jewelry, silver… everything lost to the Nazi looters. Those who were at the family home were either executed on the spot or taken to one of the concentration camps. She joined the underground where she met your ancestor. She was eventually caught by the SS and taken to one of the camps, where she met my husband's great-uncle. They survived and had a child, but they were never able to find the painting."

"What makes you think I can help? There are thought to be a hundred thousand or more art pieces still missing."

"The SS officer in charge of the raid was a man named Mühlmann. He was captured, testified against his co-conspirators, and verified the provenance of some of the recovered art. Eventually he escaped from Munich and was thought to have lived in both Bavaria and Norway, specifically around Bergen." Zofia's fingers clenched around her coffee, and she took a bracing breath. "He was involved in the *liberation* of most of the valuable artwork from the Warsaw Museum and some of the more prominent homes in the area. It is believed that he divided the cache into two or three groups, hiding one of them in the fjords outside Bergen."

Gabriella thought about how distant World War II seemed to most Americans, and yet how frighteningly close it was to many Europeans, especially those who had lost loved ones, sometimes entire families, to the Nazi death camps.

After taking a halting breath, Zofia continued, "The painting had been on loan to the Warsaw

Museum and was by Leon Wyczółkowski, entitled: A Study—The Bust of a Young Woman."

Gabriella nodded. "I know the painting. Gorgeous, evocative, and strangely enough, erotic without any nudity."

"I agree. Family legend says the woman in the painting was a member of our family."

"Is this file for me? If not, I can get someone to make copies."

"No, I made this one for you."

"Are you going to be in town for a few days? I'd like to have a chance to sit down and study what you have. If I think there's a possibility that I can recover the painting, I will."

"No, I am scheduled to go home this afternoon, but as I said, the file is yours."

"Then let's have breakfast, and you can tell me where you think this cache of Nazi treasure is located."

The waitress came and took their order, returning very quickly with it, followed by a quick visit from the chef. Sometimes it was good to be the daughter of the owner.

"Chef Andre, may I present to you my new friend Zofia Bendera." Both the chef and Zofia inclined their heads to one another. "We were both just saying how incredible the food was. I don't remember ever having better crepes, and Zofia said the eggs benedict was *magnifique*."

"I am flattered to hear you say so," said the chef. "I was a little surprised to see Mr. Jensen here in the restaurant, as he had breakfast sent up to your sister's room."

Why did it rankle that the chef thought that if Anders was visiting anyone, it was Desiree? As the thought crossed her mind, she looked down at her oversized sweater and worn jeans. Well, maybe not such a stretch of the imagination to think he was with Desi instead of her.

"The food you had delivered upstairs was outstanding. I especially enjoyed the bacon."

The chef shook his head. "Americans and their bacon."

"Yep. We do love us a good slab of hog."

The man was going to faint, she thought with a glimmer of satisfaction.

"Well," he said, "I should get back to my kitchen. I just wanted to make sure everything was to your satisfaction."

"It exceeded any and all expectations. I'll be sure to let my father know."

"*Merci, mademoiselle.*"

"Officious little bastard, isn't he?" said Zofia.

"Very. So, tell me where you think the cache might be."

"There is a place called Skjult Fjord; it means hidden fjord. It is not recorded on any official maps, but it is said to be above Kattegat…"

"Isn't there some dispute about whether a village of that name ever existed?"

"Yes, the village in the television series was fictional. Actually, the real Kattegat is an area of sea bounded by the Jutlandic peninsula, the Danish Straits, Denmark, the Baltic Sea, and Sweden. The Baltic Sea drains into the Kattegat through the Danish Straits."

"You know your bodies of water," Gabriella said with a laugh.

"Yes, both my husband and I come from a long line of fishermen. We have a sailboat in the marina outside of Bergen. We very much like to be on the water, but my husband broke from family tradition to become a policeman."

Gabriella nodded. "My family has deep roots in Louisiana, New Orleans to be specific. I understand the feeling that you need to break away from the path laid down by your parents. My family owns high-end restaurants and boutique hotels all over the world. I was raised on haute cuisine and couture. Me? I'm happy in jeans and cowboy boots eating a hotdog from a street vendor. If it hadn't been for Desi, I fear my mother would have disowned me."

"Your sister is the famous supermodel, Desiree, correct?"

"One and the same, but she'll always be Desi to me."

"You are close?"

"We are close, but we are also very different. We both diverged from the future our parents saw for us, but then took very different paths from each other. But still, there is nothing either of us wouldn't do for the other."

Gabriella signed for the bill, waving away Zofia's offer to pay, and then walked her to the entrance of the hotel. Impulsively, Gabriella hugged her. Zofia's body was stiff and resistant at first and then she hugged her back.

"I'll talk to you in a couple of days," said Gabriella.

She watched as Zofia headed out into the busy Parisian day, sensing, rather than seeing, Anders walking up behind her. It was as if she could feel not just his presence, but his essence. Gabriella didn't like the idea of making a deal where Anders got to keep one of the stolen paintings, but if it was part of a large cache, wasn't it worth it? Wasn't it true that the needs of the many outweighed the needs of the one?

Gabriella had to ask herself if she really believed that or was the real lure trying to put right a wrong from long ago? Then there was the rather large finder's fee involved, as well as a wealth of publicity and added boon to her reputation.

"Might I assume you would be interested in hearing what I have to say?" he asked, knowing full well what her answer would be.

She did not disappoint him. "I am."

CHAPTER 7

Gabriella headed back to the elevator, intending to return to her room. Anders gently grasped her elbow and headed toward the hotel's bar.

"They're not open," Gabriella said.

"Good. I don't know that we want to talk business in front of your sister, and I don't have enough information about what went down last night to feel safe having you go outside. Damn sure Desiree is not safe returning to her flat."

"You might want to check with Desi before making plans for her."

"I checked with her while you met with Zofia. She wasn't happy but I was able to persuade her to remain until I speak with the police and can ensure her safety."

"I don't mean to be rude..."

"Don't you?" he teased.

"Okay, maybe I do, but that's beside the point. I want to know why you think you are suddenly in charge of my sister's and my well-being? I appreciate your help last night, but the Paris police are on it. Desi is a relatively recognizable model in the fashion industry. Trust me, they don't want the designers, models, photographers, and the like to be all up in arms about safety. Fashion week is right around the corner so I'm sure they're making it a priority."

"Maybe, maybe not. I'm not willing to take that chance."

"Again, who asked you to? Desi and I are both capable of taking care of ourselves and really don't need your assistance. Besides which let's assume you were right about it being bratva. Isn't that the Russian mob? Aren't you a mobster? Can't you just call whoever is in charge and tell them Desi doesn't have whatever it is they want, or that you'll make them an offer they can't refuse?"

"There is no overall boss for the bratva. As with many organized crime groups, there is a kind of ruling council to which each family has a representative, but there is no one person that controls everything. Besides, most criminal organizations will not do business with the bratva. Their version of honor has to do with being slavishly devoted to those above them in their family and little else. While some other groups might go after someone who has wronged them, they will generally take care of the man's family, so they don't suffer. The bratva has a scorched earth policy and will kill the man responsible as well as every member of his immediate family and sometimes, depending on the seriousness of the offense, members of his extended family as well."

"You keep using the masculine pronoun…"

Anders chuckled again. She really needed to develop some kind of defense system against his highly seductive voice, manner, and most especially his laugh. It was deep and rich and full of mirth. He seemed to regard everything as something for his amusement.

"That is because with few exceptions, organized crime families are heavily male dominated. In most instances women are either regarded as Madonnas, fit for the raising of one's offspring, or whores, used for a man's pleasure. There's not a lot of in between."

"That's pretty misogynistic, don't you think?"

He shrugged. "Perhaps, but you asked why I used the masculine pronoun. I do not know of a single bratva family that has women in any kind of ranked position."

"What about your organization?" she challenged.

"Alas, I fear while I am not quite as unenlightened as our Russian brethren. I will not put women in the line of fire. I don't see them as only Madonnas or whores, but I was raised to believe that women were to be cherished and protected."

"And under a man's thumb." She jerked her arm away. "If, and that's a big if, we're going to work together you need to know I won't be subject to anyone's authority save my own and you and I will have a strictly professional relationship."

Anders grasped the top of her arm. "There is no 'if.' What you seek to do is going to be dangerous and there are plenty of people, the Odessa and the bratva included, willing to kill you to either stop you or to steal the artwork from you."

"Let go," she said, jerking her arm away again. "I'm warning you, Jensen. I won't be manhandled or bullied by the bratva, the Odessa, or you."

She turned to walk away and eluded his attempt to take possession of her arm again. Gabriella was not as successful the third time.

"Gabriella. Stop. You are going to listen to me, and you will do as I say so that I can keep you safe."

"Francois?" she called, and a burly man dressed in a suit approached her.

"*Mademoiselle* Broussard. I hear you and your sister are staying with us. Is there something I can do to be of service?"

"Yes, get Mr. Jensen's things from his room, tell the front desk to comp it, and show him the door."

Francois looked between Anders and Gabriella.

"Do not put your man between us, Gabriella. He is aware of who I am and that I have men stationed throughout the hotel to keep you and Desiree safe. If you like, he can remove my bag to your room as I won't be using the room and I know you are full. Now," he said, taking a deep breath and expelling it slowly as if to get a rein on his temper, "let's go into the bar and talk like adults. You need my money. I am willing to underwrite the entire cost of the project, including a substantial finder's fee for you. How many families and museums could benefit from your success?"

"All but one," she said sweetly.

He shook his head and chuckled again; his good humor restored. "*Touché.* Come along, Gabriella; you know you want to."

"No, I don't, but you make an excellent point, and I would not be acting in the best interests of my client if I didn't at least hear you out." She turned to Francois. "Go ahead and get his bag and tell the front desk that room will be open, and that Mr. Jensen didn't use it last night."

"Should I take it to the family suite?"

"No. Bring it down to the desk. He can pick it up on his way out when we're finished talking."

Again, Francois seemed concerned, and Gabriella wanted to stomp her foot in frustration but knew it would be a pointless and childish gesture.

"Do as she asks, Francois. Regardless of what happens, I can pick it up on my way out."

"Oui, *Monsieur* Jensen," replied Francois with utmost respect.

As he walked away, Gabriella sighed. "God, that was annoying."

She looked pointedly at Anders' hand, still wrapped around her upper arm, and arched her eyebrow at him. He shrugged and then steered her toward the empty bar.

"I told you I don't like being manhandled," she seethed under her breath, barely loud enough for him to hear.

"When I get to manhandling you, Rella, you will have no doubt or choice about it."

"My name is Gabriella and if you aren't careful, I'm going to insist that you call me Ms. Broussard."

"I will call you as I will. You may as well start getting used to the idea that you are, in fact, answerable to my authority. I do have contacts that can get a message to the bratva's council and will let them know that you and your sister are under my protection."

He took her to the dimmest, darkest corner of the bar, and pivoted the table out so that she could easily slide into the crescent-shaped booth.

"C'est des conneries," she swore under her breath.

"I should warn you, Rella," he said emphasizing the nickname, "I speak fluent Norwegian, English, Danish, Swedish, Russian and Italian. I don't speak much French, but I do recognize common swear words and phrases. You will be respectful in how you speak to me."

"If you actually believe that, you don't know me very well. I've been told I have issues with authority."

"Was that the general assumption at Dante's?"

Gabriella sat back, trying to put as much distance between them as the small, intimate booth allowed. She could feel her cheeks warming and was sure they were getting pink. How the hell did he know about Dante's?

"You… you know Dante's?" she stammered.

Did this mean he knew about Desi, as well? Bad enough if he told people about her, but she wasn't sure how the world would feel about a supermodel who liked to be tied to a St. Andrews cross and flogged.

"Anyone who knows anything about the upper end lifestyle clubs in Europe and Great Britain knows Dante's in Florence, Baker Street in London, and Termonn in Inverness. I have Master status at all three, and business dealings with all three owners."

"Yes, I'd heard Gavan Drummond was a gangster, too. But I thought Jordan James and Marco DeMedici were honorable, law-abiding citizens."

"Rella, quit trying to be provocative. It will not accomplish your goal. If you knew Jordan at all, you would know that her friends call her JJ and her husband insists she be referred to with his last name, Fitzwallace. Given his experience and skill in black ops, most people are not going to argue the point. Marco, on the other hand, is the best kind of scoundrel and runs his family's vineyard and other interests with an iron hand. Have you met his wife, Catherine? She has a background in art restoration. Brilliant mind. And Gavan is a good friend and a more honorable man you will never meet."

"I've never been to Baker Street. I hear it is incredible."

Anders nodded. "It is, but to get in, you need to be either the guest of a member or be invited by JJ herself. After we find the cache of stolen paintings, if you like, I'd be delighted to treat you to an evening in London. I think you would like Baker Street very much."

"*We* aren't going to do anything. I will develop a plan and execute it by myself. I work alone."

"If I am funding this little expedition, I will be involved, and you will not put yourself in danger by trying to do this alone or without backup. As I said there are members of both the Odessa and the bratva who have no desire for those paintings to ever see the light of day again."

"Why not just split the finder's fee with me?" asked Gabriella, "Why do you insist on keeping that one drawing?"

"Because it isn't the money I want. I want the drawing. It has meaning to me."

"What kind of meaning?" She sat forward on the banquette, her eyebrows arching upward as curiosity overtook her reluctance to do business with a gangster.

"I have intrigued you. Good. I will make a separate deal between just you and me. On the day you put the drawing in my hands, I will tell you why it is important."

"Tell me now."

"No."

"You can't dictate to me how I go about conducting my business."

"You are the expert in this field, I would not think of imposing myself on the scholarly side of this project. But as I am funding it, and I have no illusion that it will be an inexpensive proposition, I will insist on being kept up-to-date and being involved when I deem it necessary to keep you safe."

"You seem to think this is a done deal."

"We both know that it is. I know a little about Zofia's family history and know that she is just the sort of client you gravitate to. I also know that she and her husband do not have the money to fund your expedition. While the finder's fee would be quite large, the up front and out-of-pocket costs would be astronomical and as you refuse to use your family's money, it would prove unfeasible for you to do this without my assistance."

Gabriella had to give it to him, the man had done his research. He had outlined the predicament she found herself in. She wanted desperately to help

Zofia. It seemed like it was something she should do to honor her great-grandmother, and if she found the entire cache, it would send her reputation into the stratosphere. But he was right; the costs would be exorbitant.

"I call the shots."

"With the exception of matters of safety, and then I, and I alone, am in charge."

Anders extended his hand, and reluctantly she took it. "Why is it I get the feeling I just made a deal with the devil?"

"But such a handsome devil," he said with a laugh.

Oh, he was right about that. Gabriella could see all the ways this could, and probably would, go horribly wrong, but he had her between a rock and a hard place. She would need to wait and look for her chance to escape. What frightened her, given the magnetic pull he seemed to have for her, was when the time came, would she even want to?

CHAPTER 8

Anders escorted her back to the family suite. He knocked and was given entry by the large man standing just inside the door. As they entered, Gabriella couldn't help but laugh. Desi was stark naked eating a banana in the most provocative way.

"Do I even want to know?" Gabriella asked, laughing.

"Anders, this guy is as dull as dirt," pouted Desi prettily. "I tried to get him to come and eat *with* me and he told me he was on duty. Then, I offered to let *him eat me* and he turned me down. He's like those stupid guards at Buckingham Palace who never crack a smile. He's most annoying."

Anders shook his head and turned to his man. "Nils, you can wait outside or if you like, you can take a cold shower. I am quite sure you are not immune to Desiree's charms."

"No, Alpha, I am not. She needs…" Nils started.

"I know. Her sister isn't much better, but in an entirely different way." He turned to Desiree, shaking his finger. "As for you miss, you need to be taken in hand and have your pretty bottom spanked."

"You offering to do the job?" Desi purred at him.

He shook his head. "Not I, but I am quite sure I could find a number of volunteers."

"Why not you? Don't you like my tits?" she said, lifting them to show them to her best advantage.

"Alas, fair Desiree, my heart belongs to another," said Anders, pretty much ignoring Desi, which Gabriella knew would only encourage her.

Melodramatically grabbing a butter knife, Desi said in a firm voice, "Who is this bitch? Let me at her. I'll cut her heart out."

"You will do nothing of the sort, Desiree. Now, get dressed."

"I don't want to. I want to play," Desi wheedled, sidling up next to him and rubbing her body along his in an enticingly seductive manner.

"Desiree," he growled in a voice that revealed his dominance was not confined only to the club scene but permeated his life. "I told you to get dressed. I will count to three…"

"And then what?" Desi challenged.

"If you have not complied, I will allow my man to give your pretty bottom a discipline spanking, and then you will get dressed."

Desi stepped back from him as if his whole body had become a live wire and the electricity shocked her into moving away.

"You wouldn't dare," she whispered, but Gabriella couldn't tell if her tone was laced with fear or arousal.

"I would, and I would make sure it was not something you would want repeated. I told Gabriella downstairs that until we know what the bratva wanted with you, that you and she will be under my protection and answer to my authority."

"You touch my sister, asshole," said Gabriella, "and I will call the cops, and have you arrested so fast it'll make your head spin."

"I can tell you play at being submissive at Dante's. Do the Doms there let you top from the bottom? I guarantee you that would not be allowed at Baker Street or Termonn, and it will not happen at Sabu Stronghold."

"In case you missed it, we're not at any of those places. We're in Paris. You know what, Anders? I don't think this partnership is going to work out, after all. Take your thugs and get out. If our security personnel can't or won't do the job, I suspect Inspector Reynard Leclerc would be happy to. I've never known a straighter arrow. He doesn't even see eye to eye with me all the time, and I helped his family recover a painting that had been stolen from them when the Nazis occupied Paris."

"Leclerc?" said Desi. "Isn't he that tall, good looking bald guy?"

Gabriella smiled. "One and the same."

"Maybe he'd like to come and play with me…" Desi pouted.

Rolling her eyes, Gabriella said, "Straight shooter. Honorable. Wife and the most adorable twin girls. I'm afraid you'd be barking up the wrong tree with Leclerc. I know for a fact he hates gangsters."

"True about both gangsters and being a straight arrow," said Anders. "I've never had the pleasure of meeting his wife and little girls. But he has no love for the bratva whatsoever and even less for the Nazis. His family lost a great deal when Paris was occupied."

Desi made a sound of absolute boredom as she plopped down naked on the settee. Anders did not seem overly impressed with her sister's histrionics—whether real or play acted. He reached down to take Desi's wrist, pulling her to her feet. Thinking she was going to have her way and perhaps get the gorgeous Viking into bed, Desi purred at him. It was almost comical when Anders turned her away to point her towards the bedroom and smacked her ass with more than just a bit of sting.

"Get dressed, Desiree," he ordered, "or I will have your willful disobedience dealt with in a way you won't soon forget." Anders turned and snatched Gabriella's phone away from her. "You will behave as well."

"Or what? You'll let your man spank me?" Gabriella taunted.

"No, Rella, I will administer your spanking myself. I have had enough of both of you." He turned to Desi. "Do I need to call my man?"

Realizing she had pushed the wrong man too far, Desiree dropped her eyes. "No, Sir. I'll go get dressed. Do I have to stay in my room?"

Gabriella blinked her eyes and found it hard to speak. She was, to say at the least, shocked. She'd never, ever seen Desi act like that. Ever. Not even at Dante's.

"No. Go get dressed and then come back here and join Gabriella and me. I want to talk with you about what happened last night." He watched Desi enter the bedroom and close the door. He shook his head. "She needs the right man to take her in hand."

"I'm surprised you didn't take her up on her offer. I think you may be the first man who ever told Desi no and meant it. She isn't used to being turned down."

"Your sister is a spoiled brat who has traded on her beauty and charm, I suspect, her whole life."

"Desi isn't what you think. She's one of the kindest people I have ever known."

"I believe you, but she is also willful and arrogant, and while you would openly challenge a man, your sister would prefer to lead one around by his dick. But then she'd never respect him. She needs to belong to a man who will value her intelligence and loving nature but keep her in line. I suspect when he comes along, your sister will have trouble sitting comfortably for a while."

"As I said, I've never known Desi to back down."

"Perhaps she is not used to dealing with a truly dominant man."

"Well, don't try that shit with me; it won't work."

Anders laughed loudly. "No, I suspect it will take several trips over your Dominant's knee for you to understand you will answer to his authority. But that is a discussion better saved for another day. Do you really know Leclerc well enough to call him?"

"I do."

"Good. Call him and ask him if he's seen the report from last night. Ask him to join us here in the room for lunch. I do want to talk to Desi and if possible, I'd like to see Leclerc lead the investigation."

"Why? You don't own him."

"I don't need to. He's a brilliant investigator and as you know, is unassailable. He will find the answers, regardless of whose feathers he has to ruffle."

Gabriella tapped her index finger to her lips and said in a disbelieving voice. "You respect him."

"I do, and what I know of the man, I like and admire," admitted Anders. "I think we are far more alike than he'd care to admit, and in his own way, I think he respects me as well."

"How can a cop respect a gangster?" she asked with genuine curiosity.

"Why don't you call him and invite him for lunch. Then you can ask him."

She held out her hand and for a moment he looked at her without comprehending, then chuckled and tossed her his phone. Desi chose that moment to return to the room.

"Anders?"

"Yes, Desiree," he answered her with a smile.

"Would you mind giving your man my apologies? The attack last night was a bit unnerving, and I just had a lot of shock and adrenaline racing through my body. You were right, I was acting inappropriately."

Anders wrapped his arm around Desiree, but in a completely non-sexual way—more like an older brother comforting a beloved little sister.

"You will have a chance to do so yourself. Your sister is supposed to be calling Leclerc. I have invited him for lunch. I want you to be on your best behavior and answer all of his or my questions. Do you think you can do that for me?"

"Yes, Sir."

"Good girl. Let's see if we can get Gabriella to be a good girl as well."

Gabriella gave him a derisive snort and placed a call to the Paris police. It took a few minutes, but finally she had Leclerc on the line.

"Reynard? It's Gabriella Broussard. I'm going to

put you on speaker. I'm here at the hotel with my sister Desi and Anders Jensen."

"I was just going over the reports from last night. I understand *Monsieur* Jensen was most helpful in securing the scene and getting you and your sister to safety."

"Desi is still kind of shook up. Would it be possible for you to head up the investigation? And if so, could you join us up in our suite at the hotel for lunch? Anders thought it might be easier on Desi to answer your questions and go over what happened here."

"I had already asked for the assignment. The brass here thought given my past interactions with you, it might be easier on everyone to have a familiar face. Would one o'clock be too late?" he asked.

"No, one would be fine. Thank you, Reynard."

"Gabriella, before you hang up, do you think what happened last night could have anything to do with you?"

"I don't see how. I came up to go to the Louvre's fund-raising event. At the time, I didn't have a client and wasn't working on anything."

"And now?" asked Leclerc.

"I was engaged by a Norwegian national this morning," Gabriella said, hedging her answer.

"And would the 'Norwegian national' be Mr. Jensen?"

"No, it wouldn't, and don't ask me for a name.

You know I hold my clients' information in the strictest of confidence."

"For now, I will allow you that and believe you when you say your business had nothing to do with what happened to Desiree. But if my investigation leads me to believe otherwise, we will need to revisit the question of your client."

"Good enough."

Gabriella ended the call. "I'd like to get started on my client's project."

"The woman you met with this morning?" asked Desi. "A new stolen art piece?"

"Yes," said Gabriella.

"Was it stolen by the Nazis?" asked Desi with all the enthusiasm of a child wanting to hear their favorite storybook.

Desi always loved hearing about the things Gabriella was working on. The problem was, Desi wasn't always the most circumspect and more than once, Gabriella had ended up with either local police or Interpol interference. Generally, she wasn't breaking any laws—not major ones at least—but still, cops were cops, and they could get testy with civilians doing or finding something that they couldn't, especially if it had been right under their noses.

"Desiree," said Anders, distracting her older sister, "do you play backgammon?"

"I love backgammon, but I have to tell you, I am an excellent player."

"She is," agreed Gabriella, mouthing 'thank you' to Anders behind and over her sister's head.

"Well, we'll have to see how good you are. Is there a board up here?"

"Yes, we keep it in this ottoman," explained Desi. "Mostly this suite is reserved for family or employees, so we equipped it with things someone might need if they were here for a while and had kids with them."

"Very thoughtful. Let's get it set up and let your sister work."

Desi turned and bestowed a dazzling smile on Gabriella. "I think you're the one who stole his heart away." She turned back to Anders. "You'll need to lighten her up. She can be great fun when she wants to play, but most of the time she wants to do dull lawyerly things."

"I'll see what I can't do to change that," said Anders with a smile.

Gabriella ignored both of them and went to curl up in the window seat with the file Zofia had given her. Sitting cross-legged, Gabriella had barely begun to spread the contents of the file out before her when the window to her left shattered, spitting glass at her.

CHAPTER 9

Anders moved faster than Gabriella thought was humanly possible, pushing Desi down onto the floor before rushing to Gabriella and pulling her down, covering her body with his. The door burst open and two of his security men charged in.

"Building across the street, top floor, fourth window from the left," Anders said. "I've got them, bring the SUV around, we're getting out of here. Gabriella, you can call Leclerc when we're in the vehicle and I know we're secure."

"Leclerc had nothing to do with this," said Gabriella.

"I know that, but someone may have had his phone bugged or overheard that he was coming. If the two of you know each other and given your family's and Desiree's prominence here in Paris, it would be logical to think Leclerc would be assigned. We need to move. Desiree, you're with Nils. You stay close and do what he tells you. Rella, you're with me. Let's move."

He started to drag her forward and Gabriella tore loose from him to gather the contents of the file and shove it into her bag, right beside her laptop. He shook his head. "That's the last time you pull away from me without consequences."

The man Gabriella assumed was Nils, grabbed a stunned Desi and propelled her forward, keeping her close as they made their way down the hallway to the back stairs.

"How do you know about these stairs?" Gabriella asked Anders as they started down.

"I make it my business to know everything about any place I'm staying," he said as he kept her close and ensured his body was shielding hers and Desi's from anything approaching from behind, while Nils took point, sandwiching the two women in between them.

Gabriella was glad that the hotel was only five stories tall. Her knees hated stairs—too many years riding in upper echelon three-day event competitions had left her knees not bad to look at, but not the best for strenuous exercise involving a lot of bending and flexing of the knees.

As if he sensed her growing discomfort, Anders put his hand on her shoulder, "Are you all right?"

"I'll be fine."

He nodded and they made their way to the lower-level parking lot, where there was a limousine waiting. He ushered Nils and Desiree into the back, sitting with their backs to the driver's compartment while he directed Gabriella into the opposite seat.

"It looks as if your knees, especially the right one, is giving you trouble."

"I'll be fine, but if there's an ice pack and some kind of anti-inflammatory pills when we get to wherever we're going, I'd be grateful."

"Don't worry Rella, I'll take care of you," he purred, and she felt as if a warm cocoon was settling over her.

"I don't like being called that," she said, far more sharply than she'd intended.

He brushed his lips against the side of her temple. "Fine. I will ensure no one but me calls you that, and then only when we are alone."

"Who was shooting at us?" asked Desiree, whose face had lost all of its color.

"They were most likely shooting at Anders, Desi."

"No," he said. "they were not. Had they been shooting at me, the shot would have been much higher. No, they were aiming either for you or Desiree. My men will see if they can't find who it was. May I borrow your mobile?"

Gabriella handed it to him, and he quickly dialed Leclerc.

"Inspector Leclerc, this is Anders Jensen, and you

are on speaker with myself, one of my men, and the Broussards."

"Are you calling about the shot fired at the hotel?"

"I am. I have the girls with me, and we will be leaving Paris."

"Not if I have anything to say about it."

"You don't," growled Anders. "Either you or someone in your department are compromised. Given what I know of you, I would guess the latter."

"Just because someone takes a shot at you."

"I think when you look at where the bullet came through the glass, you will see that they were aiming for one of the girls. When I have them safe, I will call you on a secure line and give you our location."

"Listen Jensen, this is a police matter. Bring them to headquarters."

"No," said Anders before removing the battery and the SIM card and tossing both them and the phone itself out the window where they were quickly crushed by Parisian traffic. He turned to Nils. "Have them ready the plane for immediate takeoff."

"Already done," said Nils.

"That was my phone," said Gabriella. "It was new."

"I will buy you an even better one," replied Anders, craning his neck and showing the first signs of stress on his handsome features.

"Tell me, just out of interest," started Gabriella, "do all of your men look like they could have stepped out of a historical Viking romance novel? Seriously, all Nils here needs is an appropriate costume and a shield and sword."

Nils chuckled and Desi giggled. "You'll have to forgive Gabi. When she's scared she tends to babble about inappropriate things."

"I don't know, Desi, look at him. I'm sure I've seen him on your Kindle."

Desi took a hard look at Nils. "You know, you might be right. So why couldn't I get him to pillage me earlier? Or would that be plundering?"

"Desiree," warned Anders, "the plane has comfortable seats but not so comfortable that it will accommodate a well-spanked backside without some degree of discomfort."

"You wouldn't do that to me, would you Nils?" Desi said, batting her eyes at him.

"Desiree, enough or you will face discipline," Anders growled at her in what Gabriella was beginning to think of as his sexy Viking Dom voice.

They sped out of Paris and were at the airport, loaded into Anders' private jet and taxiing down the runway before the Paris police could even begin to try and set up roadblocks. They took off and banked northeast towards Norway, flying under the radar. Whoever this pilot was, he was good and Gabriella suspected this was not the first time he'd smuggled his boss out of a country with the police hot on their tails.

Once they were settled, Anders moved back to take a seat by himself. He needed some space from Gabriella. She was too smart by half, and he didn't need her questioning him. Desiree was another concern. She needed to be taken in hand and Anders was tempted to let Nils discipline the beautiful blonde, but not until he had more information about what was happening. Disciplining unmated females was the job of either their alpha or their beta. While Nils might well be the clan's beta, Desiree was not a member of their clan nor was she a shifter—although he had begun to think that if Nils had his way, that might not be the case for too much longer. Besides, Anders was going to have his hands full with his own beautiful fated mate, Gabriella.

His mind was full of questions, none of which he could indulge until they were secure on the plane and headed for Norway. He would take them to his stronghold, Sabu. His pilot was intelligent enough to call ahead and ensure his people knew two humans would be with him.

But why had the bratva gone after Desiree? And was the shot fired from the sniper rifle intended for Desiree or Gabriella? Anders circled back to why. What could Desiree be involved with that would make the bratva want to harm her? He could well imagine any number of ways Gabriella could have provoked someone into trying to shoot her. But who and why? And was the attack on Gabriella tied to the attack on Desiree in some way? Could it be that the attack on Desiree had been made as a warning or a way to get at Gabriella? Perhaps what had happened to Desiree had nothing to do with Desiree at all.

He realized how distracted he was when Gabriella settled comfortably with a Diet Coke in hand in the seat opposite him.

"I can see the wheels spinning," said Gabriella.

Anders nodded slowly and thoughtfully. "Too many questions and not enough answers. What bothers me is I don't think we have enough information to even be asking the right questions."

"You're sure the shot wasn't meant for you?"

"Wrong angle and far too low to be effective. I want to think it was meant for Desiree, but I don't think it was."

"Me? Who would want to kill me? And why?"

"I have no idea. And if it was you and not Desiree, are the two incidents connected? If not, then we have two separate mysteries."

"I get the feeling you aren't big on not knowing the answers to things."

Anders smiled. "You have good instincts. I've stayed alive and kept my people safe mostly by relying on mine. This, whatever it is, isn't over."

"Can I ask where you're taking us?"

"You will be guests in my home, Sabu, up above Bergen on the western coast of Norway."

"Guests or prisoners?" she asked, pointedly.

"Whatever makes you feel better. You will stay within the walls of the stronghold. I know we left with not so much as a toothbrush for either of you. Once we have you installed in your rooms, if you'll make a list of what you need and your sizes, I'll send someone into Bergen to get whatever it is you want."

"That's kind of you, and I'll feel better knowing that Desi is safe with you."

"You will both be safe with me. Settle yourself with the idea that you will be at Sabu until I deem it safe for you to leave."

"You can't just whisk us off and hold us against our will. That's kidnapping, you know, and combined with leaving the country and given who you are, I suspect Interpol will get involved."

"You are, no doubt, right about that," he said.

"And that doesn't bother you?"

"Not much when we were still in Paris, less now that we are en route to Norway, and not at all once we reach Sabu. Did you know that my family has occupied the stronghold since the age of the Vikings and in all of that time, its walls have never been breached, nor has any siege been successful?"

"No," she said, shaking her head, "I didn't know that."

"I'll let you share my office with me. It's large, comfortable, and has a commanding view."

"I don't give a shit about the view. How's your internet?"

Anders laughed. "Excellent. We have our own satellite."

"Seriously?" she asked.

"Seriously," he assured her.

Leaning back in his seat, he admired the way her red hair fell in loose curls past her shoulders. He could see why Desiree was the model—tall, willowy, blonde hair and blue eyes—she was stunningly beautiful. Almost too perfect for Anders' way of thinking. His Gabriella wasn't much shorter but had a far more curvaceous figure. She had an interesting, intelligent, and pretty face, large firm breasts, a smaller waist, and generous hips a man could use to his advantage when he fucked her. Her legs were long and well formed.

He didn't question the fact that he already referred to her as 'his Gabriella,' as that was the way he thought of her. She was beautiful, intelligent, skilled, resourceful, and fairly fearless. Most women, had they been shot at and had a bullet pass that close to them, would have been dithering idiots. Gabriella had merely done what she needed to do.

She was going to make the most hauntingly beautiful snow leopard anyone had ever seen.

Desiree's reaction had been curious as well. He

would have expected her to be even more unnerved than her sister. Anders wasn't quite sure he bought her vapid blonde act as there was far too much intelligence in her eyes. He wondered what secrets she was hiding.

Until he knew more about both of them, he meant to keep a close eye on them, and what better way to do that than keeping them safe at Sabu.

CHAPTER 10

The plane dropped down so close to the ocean, Gabriella was certain if they could open a window, she could reach out and touch it. They flew up the coastline of Norway and made good time.

"How long has your castle been there?" Gabriella asked him.

"I don't know that anyone knows. My family seized the stronghold during the age of the Vikings, helping to establish and build the city into a major trading port. We have lived in continual residence since that time."

Gabriella turned to him. "That's rather unusual, isn't it? Don't castles, palaces, fortresses and the like change hands on a fairly regular basis?"

"It depends on the country and the family holding the territory. I know of several families throughout

Europe who have been in residence for more than a thousand years," answered Anders.

What he didn't add was that in every instance of which he was aware, the family was not entirely human.

"Wasn't Bergen also the port that the Shetland Bus operated out of?"

Desi perked up. "They had a bus for ponies?"

Anders chuckled. "Not Shetland ponies, but rather their homeland, the Shetland Islands."

"But those are Scottish. How could a bus run from Norway to Scotland?"

"They didn't use buses," explained Nils. "Norwegian fishermen worked with the British military to smuggle arms, money, people, and information between Norway and Scotland. They helped a great many British expatriates who had been living in Norway to get home, as well as getting British spies into the country so they could infiltrate Germany."

"It's believed a few high-ranking Nazi officers managed to sneak their way on board. A couple were exposed during the trip and never made it to Scotland," supplied Gabriella.

"There are tales of the Nazis building vaults in some of the larger cavern systems in the fjords to hide gold, jewels, and paintings," explained Anders.

"Do you believe the paintings from the Warsaw Museum ended up in these vaults?" asked Gabriella.

"Not all of them, and not all in one place. The

Nazis stole so much, not just from museums, but from individuals as well. There are more than one hundred thousand pieces, that we know of, that are still missing. You can fault the Nazis for a great many things, and do not think for a minute I have anything good to say about them, but they were excellent recordkeepers. In the end, it was their downfall. They were so anxious to preserve what they saw as their glorious conquering of the world, they wrote everything down."

"They occupied Bergen for most of the war, didn't they?" asked Gabriella.

Anders nodded. "They did. It was an important port for them, which is why the Shetland Bus is so impressive. They worked literally right under the Nazis' noses."

Gabriella was very interested in the area's history. Anders Jensen might well prove to be an excellent resource, but did she really want to do business with a gangster? He had made a good point, though, of being able to underwrite a large project to reunite people with their stolen art, if only she could find it.

"Did any of them ever occupy Sabu?" she asked.

He chuckled. "They tried. It did not go well. They decided the stronghold was haunted by demons and in the end told their high command it was impractical. The fact is, my family managed to kill some of them and get rid of the bodies so it was as if they just disappeared."

"Yah," said Nils. "Except for that one SS patrol."

"What happened to them?" asked Desi.

Gabriella was surprised at Desi's interest, which seemed real, rather than feigned. Normally she had no use for anything that didn't have to do with fashion.

"The SS wanted to prove that the regular officers were cowards," continued Nils, "so they came up to the stronghold to seize it. There were seven men. When the regular army commander sent a search party for them, they found them dead, stuffed with straw, impaled on poles and posed like scarecrows. The Nazis never bothered those at Sabu again."

Anders nodded. "Our people operated a fairly active cell of the Norwegian underground and resistance, often hiding high value targets until they could be taken to safety."

"That's fascinating," said Desi, batting her eyes at Nils.

"Your sister needs to be spanked," whispered Anders to Gabriella. "And if she's not careful Nils is going to accommodate her."

"You should know, Desi likes impact play."

"But there is an enormous difference between being bound to a St. Andrew's cross and flogged for arousal or relaxation and having a dominant male take you to task over his knee for discipline."

"If he hurts my sister," Gabriella said sweetly, "I'll cut his nuts off and feed them to him with a spoon."

Anders laughed. "You will do no such thing, my sweet Rella. Your sister will learn who is dominant and who is submissive. I am surprised you are the younger sister."

So, he'd done some research, had he?

"I am not your sweet anything and stop calling me that. As for Desi and me, she's always taken after the French side of our family. I'm far more like my Cajun ancestors. You ought to taste my jambalaya. Some of the best in Louisiana."

"I will look forward to that."

The plane circled the City of Bergen before flying up to the bluff where the impressive Sabu Stronghold sat, keeping watch over the city. It wasn't as fancy as a lot of castles, but it was strong and proud, and Gabriella could well imagine Anders' family terrorizing the Nazis from its lofty position.

"Your home is beautiful," she said as they approached the landing strip.

"You and your sister have an open invitation to stay as long as you like. I would suggest it would make an excellent base for your search, but it would sound self-serving."

"Self-serving, how?" she asked, confused.

"I would have you stay here with me, forever."

Gabriella rolled her eyes. "You really are the most annoying man. Don't you have the bratva to fight off? You can't romance someone at night and then go off to murder people during the day."

"I assure you, I can kill my enemies and still keep you safe and happy. It is not murder when you are protecting your own, especially where the bratva is concerned."

They landed and Gabriella was surprised to see two large, horse-drawn carriages waiting for them. She thought she recognized the man standing next to one of the carriages, who walked up as the plane rolled to a stop and the staircase was let down.

Anders walked off first, embracing the man. "Gabriella, you remember Sig."

"I don't think we were formally introduced, but welcome to the Sabu Stronghold," he said.

"What's with the carriages?" asked Desi.

Nils took her arm, hooking it through his. "Anders is a bit of a romantic. He often prefers to take the carriage down from the plane to the bailey—that's the kind of large courtyard in the keep. It's big enough for four. I'm sure he wouldn't mind if we rode with them, would you Anders?"

"Not at all. I do prefer the carriages, and as Gabriella has ridden most of her life, I thought she might prefer it, as well. We have an entire breeding program devoted to Norwegian Coldblood Trotters and Norwegian Dole Horses."

"These are Trotters, right?" said Gabriella walking up and offering her hand to the beautiful silver-coated horse with a pure black mane, tail, and points.

"You know your breeds. The best way to explore the fjords is either by horseback or on foot. You are more than welcome to ride any of the horses we have here."

"Thank you. I might take you up on that."

Anders and Nils helped them up into the carriage. Once they were settled, the driver clucked to the two horses pulling the carriage and headed down to the stronghold. Gabriella had to admit this was probably the most romantic thing she'd ever done, which said nothing good about the state of her love life.

She watched Anders from the corner of her eye as she glanced around his magnificent estate. She could see pastures and fields and large tracts of open land that led down to what appeared to be a private beach.

Gabriella looked down the tree lined drive toward what she was sure was an enormous gate. They entered over a massive bridge, passing through the imposing gate. The estate was surrounded by an impressive stone wall on three sides. The fourth side was bounded by the rustic cliff and the sea below.

"Is that the drive your people lined with the Nazi scarecrows?"

Anders nodded. "I am told it was a terrifying sight."

"I can imagine. Maybe you ought to tell the bratva that story."

Anders chuckled. "Trust me, Gabriella, they know. Sabu Stronghold is famous or infamous, depending on your point of view, for that and many other lurid and fantastical tales."

Once inside the walls of the castle, it was as if she'd been transported into some kind of magical fairyland. It was quiet enough that you could hear the breeze as it wove its way in and out of the buildings and the sea as it crashed against the rocks below.

"Motorized vehicles are not allowed past the airstrip. We taxi down deliveries by horse drawn vehicles and people either walk, ride a horse, or ride in a carriage. If we have visitors, we send the carriages for them either to the gate at the end of the drive where they can park, or up to our private airstrip."

"What if they come by boat?" Desi said, standing up until Nils pulled her back down.

"Generally, they walk up to the castle from the beach," Nils answered her, "but we also provide horses to ride. If neither of those is possible, we do have a carriage that is equipped with tires that work well in sand."

The carriage rolled to a stop and a man Gabriella assumed was the butler or majordomo came out as did friends and family to greet them.

"Dagmar," said Anders.

"Sir. I have prepared rooms for the ladies, as you requested. Should I send one of the flatbed wagons to fetch their luggage?"

Anders laughed. "I'm afraid we had to leave in such a hurry that they have nothing but the clothes on their backs. I will send someone to pick up their identification papers in Paris. Gabriella should have a bag, but someone will need to pack for Desiree. In the meantime, have someone here get their sizes and go into Bergen to get them a few things." He turned to Nils. "I don't want either of the girls leaving Sabu without an escort and my permission."

"You're bordering on prisoner versus guest," said Gabriella.

"I am ensuring your safety, as I said I would," responded Anders.

"If I may, Sir, the clan has gathered and dinner awaits you in the dining hall," said Dagmar, who, except for the Norwegian accent, could have been played by John Gielgud and appeared to be the perfect English butler.

"Thank you. Let's not keep everyone waiting, unless of course you are too tired. If so, I can have something sent up to you," Anders said solicitously.

"Gabi can be rather dull, but I say if there's a party, let's get to it," said Desi, trotting up the wide stone steps as if she owned the place.

"I'll stay with her and keep her out of trouble," offered Nils.

Anders nodded. "See that you do. I am putting you in charge of her safety and her behavior."

Nils grinned. "Understood, Alpha. I will not let you down."

"Of that I have no doubt."

As Nils jogged up the steps to catch up with Desi, Gabriella looked up at him. "You might want to tell him what I said about his nuts and a spoon."

"You'd best behave yourself, Gabriella, or Desi will not be the only one who finds herself on the receiving end of what I suspect is some much-needed discipline."

Gabriella looked at him incredulously. Had he really just said that to her? She looked around before she took Anders' proffered arm and wondered if she and Desi might not have fallen down the proverbial rabbit hole.

CHAPTER 11

It was as if they had stepped back in time or into Dracula's castle. Gabriella knew there had to be electric lights, but all she could see were candles.

"I had the lighting designed so that it fit the castle and didn't stick out like a sore thumb," Anders said, as if he was reading her mind. "The candles aren't wax; they are like the ones they use in movies."

"They're beautiful."

He nodded. "And practical. Well, practical now that it's done. It was a nightmare getting it done, but several of my people apprenticed with those we brought in from London and New York and now we are called on to do a lot of this kind of thing for movies shot here in Scandinavia."

When they entered the large dining hall, the feeling of having traveled back in time was even more pronounced. There were numerous large, rough-hewn tables with a mixture of benches and individual seating. It looked as if all those who lived and worked at Sabu also took their meals here.

"Do you feed everybody?" she asked.

"Yes, I find it easier and it promotes a feeling of teamwork and family. Here at Sabu, we care for one another as our ancestors did. Even those who work in Bergen but live up here normally take their meals here. We also have a large house in town where some of our younger people live, and then, of course, people are welcome to have their own individual homes."

"It's absolutely stunning."

He led Gabriella to what she thought would be termed the 'high table,' as it sat on a raised dais and had individual chairs. Huge fireplaces burned at either end of the hall.

"No central heat and air?" she asked.

"I may be a romantic, but I like my creature comforts. There is central heat and air. The larger guest suites have their own gas fireplaces, more for ambiance than anything else. They also have an attached bath. I believe both of you have views of the ocean. If you'd like something else, you have but to ask."

"What if I just want a ride back to Paris?"

Anders shook his head slowly. "That I cannot

allow until we know more about whoever took a shot at you."

"I am not yet convinced whoever it was, wasn't shooting at you."

"Then you are being stubborn," he said with a smile. "It was the wrong height and angle for me to have been the intended victim and the sniper would have had difficulty targeting Desiree. No, you were the one who was supposed to die. Until I find out why and who was behind it, you will remain here at Sabu."

"Leclerc…"

"If Inspector Leclerc wishes to speak with you, he is welcome to call."

He had led her up the stairs onto the dais and was holding out her chair.

"What if I tell him we were taken against our will?"

"You won't."

"You can't be sure of that."

"I can," he said, smiling down at her before taking the seat next to her. "You are far too intrigued about the possibility of getting back that cache of stolen artwork, and you know I am right about the shooter. If nothing else, you will stay here in order to keep Desiree safe."

Gabriella looked down the table to Desi who was thoroughly enjoying flirting outrageously with Nils. "I'm pretty damn sure Nils would be happy to keep Desi under his personal protection."

Anders chuckled. He seemed to find most things she said amusing. "I think you might be right about that. I know that technically you are younger than Desiree, but you must admit you are the more mature."

"*Comme ci, comme ça.* I'll let you in on a little secret," she said leaning closer to him. Anders responded by leaning into her as well. "Desi only plays at being the vapid blonde. She's a whole lot smarter than most people give her credit for."

"I wouldn't have thought that until I saw how attentive Nils is. He too is often mistaken for not being as bright as he is, and ditzy blondes hold little interest for him."

"What about his boss?"

"He is a rather discerning man. He prefers a more curvaceous woman with red curls and hazel eyes." Gabriella sat back. The last thing she needed was for some mafia kingpin to decide she should be his girl. Anders leaned back as well but continued as if he hadn't noticed. "As my right-hand man, he works hard at maintaining the security of our people and insists on traveling with me. However, your sister might prove to be just the thing to keep him closer to home."

"Something of a tomcat, is he?"

"I would not say that, but he has enjoyed the company of many women, always honestly and usually within a club setting."

"That seems rather stifling and narrow-minded," she said, watching the extraordinarily attractive couple. "He could be a model."

"He has had offers, but prefers his life here, which I thank God for. And isn't that what you American's say is the pot calling the kettle black? Neither you nor your sister date, instead finding what you need in lifestyle clubs, but you want to look down on Nils for doing the same. Don't we both find that having something spelled out in a contract can help keep things clear, so everyone knows what to expect?"

"Touché. I just worry about her. I think the grind of Paris is starting to wear her down."

"I can understand that. Paris can be an exhausting city just as a visitor. I can't imagine what it must be like to be one of its most recognizable faces. But let us leave your sister in Nils' capable hands. Should I assume you are interested in my proposition?"

"If we're talking about your business proposal, I am at least open to hearing what you have to say. But tell me, what is it about the Durer's Lioness that speaks to you so strongly that you are willing to underwrite something like this, but refuse to return it to its rightful owner?"

"We have a rule at Sabu, we do not discuss business at mealtimes. Meals are to be enjoyed and savored. We can discuss it in the morning."

"What if I don't want to wait until morning?"

"Then you will be disappointed and cross with me, which would make me very sad."

Gabriella realized he wasn't going to be baited and he had no intention of discussing the specifics with her until he chose to do so.

"So, what do you do here at Sabu?"

"It is the unofficial headquarters of Sabu Enterprises. We maintain a corporate office in Oslo, but most of those who work for the company work out of here."

"And what does Sabu do exactly?"

"We are a diversified company involved in the import/export business, as well as the energy industry—oil, natural gas, and hydropower. We also have mining and lumber interests."

"Don't you own several deep-sea rigs in the North Sea?"

He wasn't the only one who'd done some research.

He inclined his head. "Sabu owns two deep-sea rigs in the North Sea and has interests in two more, plus a new mega rig in the Gulf of Mexico. We are thinking of expanding our business in New Orleans, including both oil and seafood."

"Aren't those two kind of contradictory given the damage an oil spill can have on the environment?"

"Not at all. I believe those of us who have a foot in both camps, so to speak, can help bridge a conversation beyond the rhetoric. The deep-sea rigs can be safe. The majority never have a problem. It is up to those of us in the oil industry to ensure our rigs are safe and don't pollute our water resources. And the seafood producers need to find a way to work with the oil producers to protect their own industry. You know New Orleans, don't you? Perhaps you could show me around."

"You know that I base my business out of Nice."

"But when you…"

"If I…"

"When you," he corrected, grinning at her, "accept my proposal, it really will be much easier for you to base out of Norway, and I can put the resources of Sabu at your disposal."

"Why does the Durer mean so much to you?"

"I find the languid form of the lioness to be sensual and erotic. I have the perfect place for it in either my study or my bedroom."

"You would display a stolen piece of art?"

"Why have it if I can't look at it? If I pay to recover it, am I not entitled to it?

Gabriella shook her head. "No. There is really no statute of limitations regarding artwork stolen by the Nazis. If a claimant, in this case Warsaw University, files a claim against you within a certain period, it will be considered. It's been fairly well documented and accepted the print was stolen from them by the Nazis. I'm having some trouble deciding how I would handle this ethically and not tell them it was one of the items I recovered."

Anders shrugged. "It is of little consequence."

"Little consequence? The thing would be worth millions."

"So, your finder's fee would be…?"

"Substantial," she said, not wanting to give him a specific amount.

He shook his head with a rueful smile. "And here I am disregarding my own rules."

"I wouldn't think the leader of an organized crime syndicate would be bothered with following the rules, especially those of his own making."

"You would be wrong. Leaders of whatever ilk must lead by example. Leading by intimidation isn't leading at all, in my opinion."

"True, but what would stop the university from trying to recover their painting from you?"

"They are welcome to try, but they would need to compensate me for my loss, which would include your substantial finder's fee and the cost of recovery."

"Which given the state of Poland's economy, might not be possible."

"And," he said leaning over to her, "I suspect a charitable donation to the university might not be amiss and help them get over their loss."

"Did you really just tell me you would bribe them to go away?" she asked, trying to process both his audacity and his chances of success, which she had to admit were good.

"No, I merely suggested that the University of Warsaw might well be willing to accept a cash settlement in lieu of having a small drawing returned to them. After all, I believe they had more than the Durer drawing stolen, and the rest would be returned to them." He chuckled, shaking his finger at her. "You are a bad influence on me, Gabriella. I will not speak to you about this matter again until after we've eaten. We can sit down in my study and discuss it then."

"But…"

"But nothing," he said with an air of finality, and then began to engage her in a general conversation about her work and how she had arrived at her profession.

Gabriella was able to answer Anders' questions while keeping an eye on Desi, who seemed to have gone from flirtatious to enchanted. She and Nils were keeping their conversation low, and their body posture appeared to reflect a burgeoning intimacy. She would need to remind Desi that regardless of how attractive or attentive Nils was, he was still a gangster.

What was Desi thinking?

She twisted in her seat at the discomfort the thought suddenly raised. For that matter… what was *she* thinking?

CHAPTER 12

After dinner, many people split off from the main group to pursue their own interests. Nils had almost drawn Desi outside with him when Gabriella attempted to catch up with them. Before she could split them up, Anders prevented her from reaching them.

"Your sister plays backgammon; do you?"

"Not as well as Desi. I always preferred chess."

"Excellent. I have a beautiful chess set in my study. Perhaps you would offer me a game?"

"I thought I'd get my sister."

"Nils is taking care of Desiree. She is in the best of hands, and he will see to all her needs."

"That's what I'm afraid of," said Gabriella, shifting from one foot to the other as she tried to decide whether to go or stay.

"Come, Gabriella. Let them be."

"I do not want my sister to get involved with a gangster. That's the last thing she needs."

"I fear the ship has sailed on that; besides I believe Nils might well be the best thing that ever happens to her."

Whirling around to face him, she said, "How can you say that? She doesn't need to be known as the model with a gangster boyfriend."

"I think you misjudge the situation. I have known Nils my entire life. There is no one I trust more. He would never allow anything bad to happen to your sister. Desi is in good hands."

"Nuts. Spoon," she murmured, provoking Anders' sexy chuckle.

He led her into his study. The room was a bibliophile's dream. Bookcases filled with leather bound tomes, most of which she suspected were first editions. There was an enormous antique desk with a matching chair, two wingback chairs facing the desk, a chesterfield sofa with an ornately carved coffee table, and a window seat by the large arched window that dominated the wall overlooking the town. Behind the sofa was a chess table and chairs. The man took his game seriously. But it was the padded window seat that drew her attention. Gabriella could easily imagine curling up in the window seat with either a good book or her laptop while Anders worked at his desk.

Wait! Where had that thought come from? It was at once intriguing, disconcerting, and erotic. The image in her mind's eye had been so clear, and yet she wasn't the least bit attracted to him. Okay, so maybe she was attracted. After all, the guy was sexy as hell, but if her sister didn't need a gangster for a boyfriend, she needed one even less.

For the next few hours, Anders engaged Gabriella in an intricate game of chess. Her father had taught her the game as a small child and she became aware at an early age that if she wanted her father's attention, the best way was to give him a challenging game.

Over the course of the game, she had been sure she had him beat, until he turned things around and she feared being bested by him. In the end, they agreed to a draw.

"Excellent game," said Anders. "Can I get you a brandy?" he asked, rising from the table, and going to the bar that had been built into one of the bookcases. She liked it. It was discreet, functional, and had been done by a master craftsman.

She vaguely heard the sound of the front door opening. Before he could stop her this time, Gabriella left his study and his almost hypnotic presence looking for her sister. Nils was escorting her up the stairs to what Gabriella assumed was either her room or his. Somehow, she sensed that Nils had quarters here in the main keep.

Spotting them stopped in front of the door, she meant to rush to Desi, but stopped as Nils lowered his head to hers, brushing his lips against Desi's and whispering something that made her smile and her body go soft and relaxed against his. It wasn't some full on hard-core erotic kiss as foreplay, but there was definitely a sensual feeling to it.

"In the morning," he whispered to her as Gabriella joined them.

"Is this my sister's room?" Gabriella asked him.

"Yes. Mine is adjacent to it at this end of the hall. Anders' room is at the other end and yours is adjacent to his."

Arching her eyebrow, she asked, "Connecting doors?"

"Gabriella, be nice," admonished Desi.

"I said adjacent, Gabriella, not adjoining." He put his finger under Desi's chin and tilted her head back so that she was gazing like a lovesick virgin into the eyes of her romantic hero. "Your sister is only being protective of you."

"I need no protection from you," Desi purred.

Nils chuckled. Did Norwegian men have some kind of gene in their DNA that made their chuckles so deep and sexy?

"No, but your sister doesn't understand that yet. But you do, don't you, little one?"

"I do."

Desi was practically fawning all over this guy. Sure, he was hot, but Desi had dated dozens of hot men and when they went to Dante's she had to beat off gorgeous guys with a stick.

"Desi? I need to talk to you," said Gabriella.

"Honestly, Gabi, you have the worst timing. I was going to try to seduce Nils into joining me in either his bed or mine."

Again, with the chuckle that practically oozed sexuality. "Behave yourself, Desiree. You need to sleep, and I need to meet with Anders."

"You'll speak with him tonight?"

"Yes, little one. I told you there is nothing to worry about. A mere formality."

"So, tomorrow?"

She could practically see the purr Nils emanated wrapping its silken tendrils around Desi. "Tomorrow. Gabriella, don't keep your sister up too late. She needs her rest. I will see you in the morning, little one. Go to sleep and dream of me."

He kissed Desi's hand and nodded toward Gabriella. Ick! The guy was over-the-top in courtly manners. Surely Desi wasn't being taken in by all of that. Desi, her gorgeous, vivacious sister was smarter than that, right?

Desi reached back to open the door with one hand while she waggled her fingers at Nils with the other before blowing him a kiss, which he caught and placed on his lips before Desi slipped inside, followed by Gabriella.

When she closed the door behind her, Gabriella made a gagging sound and then mimicked throwing up. "Shit, Desi. Really?"

"Yes, really," she snapped.

Could Desi actually be serious about Nils? She'd barely known the man twenty-four hours. Could her intelligent, talented, and beautiful sister actually be falling for this guy?

"You do remember he's a thug, right?" Gabriella asked exasperated.

"He is no such thing. He is absolutely wonderful. Did you notice how he said I needed my rest and not my beauty sleep?"

Gabriella knew that being valued only, or at least most highly, for her looks was a source of contention with Desi. So many people, including all of the men she had dated, had never been able to move beyond how gorgeous she was.

"Actually, I didn't. I was kind of forced to focus on how attracted you seemed to each other."

"Attracted?" Desi giggled. "If you only saw it as attracted, you either weren't paying attention or I've lost my touch. I so wanted to jump his bones and have him fuck me all night. But he said no because we were under Anders' roof, and he needed to speak to him before courting me. He told me I had nothing to worry about because Anders is a great guy and if he decided he wanted to be an asshole, Nils would just walk away and come back to Paris with me."

"And if Anders is okay with your relationship with Nils?"

"Then we'll go back and get all my things and put my flat up for sale."

"Are you kidding me? You'd move here?"

"To be with Nils? So fast it would make your head spin. He said if I want, I can continue my modeling career and just base out of here, but I'm not sure I don't want to go out on top…"

"What the hell else would you do?"

Desi harumphed and sent her sister a pouty look. "You're not the only one with a college degree, little sister."

Desiree was right, she had a degree in architecture from Tulane and had graduated early and with honors. She had fended off several lucrative offers in lieu of her modeling career, as she knew she could make far more money. Her plan had always been to someday use her degree in restoration work.

Gabriella pulled out the desk chair and sat down. "Shit, Desi. You're serious about this guy. I mean, I get it. He's a hunk and a half, but I guess I always thought when you wanted to leave modeling, you'd stay in Paris and do something in fashion. I know several designers have asked you about that."

"No. That was never something I saw myself as doing. I hadn't thought much past that, but fashion was always just a way to make money. I'd like to do something meaningful. I mean you go around the world finding people's lost or stolen art and give it back to them. I always thought I'd either find a way to get you to let me join you or actually use my degree in architecture to create and restore some lasting beauty."

"I had no idea you even had any interest in my work."

"That's what you get for never wanting to stay in my flat. I have an entire scrapbook filled with all of the pictures and articles written about you. I may be more recognizable on the street, but your fame and reputation far exceed mine."

Gabriella laughed as she shook her head. "I never knew. Do you ever think mom and dad wondered where they went wrong?"

"All the time. It's a good thing Marc loves the family business."

"Mama would point out his name is Marcel."

"Which he quit using about the time the boys in his gym class started beating him up," reminded Desi with a smile.

Marc, or Marcel Broussard, was the middle child of the family and had been learning the business from the time his parents had allowed him to come to the office. Marc had attended Cornell University with a degree in hospitality management, and later obtained another degree from the Culinary Institute of America as a chef. There was no part of the restaurant or hotel business Marc didn't know.

"Did you know Anders graduated from the Cordon Bleu in Paris?"

"Good thing, because you can't cook worth a damn, except for your jambalaya."

"Neither can you," retorted Gabriella.

"Not true. I am an excellent cook. I just don't eat, so why bother. I swear, I've been on a diet, or as mama liked to say, 'watching my figure' since I was nine."

Gabriella wished that wasn't true, but knew it was. She reached out to squeeze Desi's hand. "I'm sorry."

Desi shrugged. "She meant well. She always knew I had a big career ahead of me."

"And you didn't disappoint."

"Yes, but it gets harder and harder to look young enough to be what designers, photographers and editors want. I've always thought it was so sad when a model passed her prime but tried to hang on."

"Don't make any rash decisions just because you're contemplating leaving modeling."

"You don't get it. I'm in love with Nils. Honest-to-God, soulmate, forever and ever love with the man and I know it makes no sense, but I don't care."

Taken aback, Gabriella wasn't quite sure what to say. "If you're sure."

"I am, but more importantly, so is he. Thus, why it's so important he talk to Anders." She laughed and Gabriella noticed that Desi had genuinely laughed more in the past twenty-four hours than she had in a very long time.

"If you're happy, then I'm happy for you. He seems like a great guy."

"He is and he's so dominant. He told me as we were walking through the gardens… oh, my God, Gabi, you must see the gardens, they're gorgeous. And when the sun goes down, they have these little fairy lights hidden amongst the plants, trees, and flowers. They even have some that bloom only at night. It's magical."

"So, he got past the banana thing?" Gabriella recalled walking in on Desi when she had been deliberately provocative with Nils, eating a banana, trying to taunt him.

"Absolutely. He did tell me if I ever teased him like that again, he'd spank me before he fucked me raw. Almost made me want to go find one."

Gabriella chuckled. It was good to see Desi so happy. Of course, she meant to find out everything she could about Nils.

"I think I'll turn in." She got up and gave her sister a hug. "I'll see you in the morning."

She left Desi and wandered down to her room. The door was open, and her duffle bag was sitting in the middle of the bed. She entered the room, closing and locking the door behind her. Although she preferred to sleep in the nude, she did keep a fine batiste nightgown in her suitcase. It was almost see-through and hid little from anyone who might see her. Still, she felt it was appropriate to have one with her.

Undressing and slipping into her nightgown, she strolled over to the window that overlooked a small strip of beautifully manicured lawn leading to a craggy precipice and path to the beach and sea below. What she saw, she knew would change her life forever.

CHAPTER 13

Anders stood on the edge of the cliff overlooking the sea and inhaled deeply, trying to clear his head. It had been more than twenty-four hours since he had first breathed in her scent. Gabriella was his fated mate and he needed to give some thought as to how to convince her of that. He wasn't overly concerned because he knew if she refused to be wooed, he would simply claim her and keep her at his side until she came to accept the idea that they were inevitable. It would make things simpler, and more enjoyable, though, if she embraced her destiny as he did.

Humans could be damned difficult sometimes.

"I thought I might find you here," said Nils, as he joined him.

Anders grinned as he shot him a look over his shoulder. "And I thought I'd either find you in a similar state or hear the yowling of your mate as you claimed her."

Nils grinned back. "I wanted to ask your permission first, Alpha," his beta said, formally.

"And if I said no?"

"Then I would leave the clan to build a life with her."

"What if she wants to leave or can't handle the truth of who we are?"

"She can. I told her before I asked her to marry me."

Anders had known Nils was smitten by the beautiful Desiree, but this was something of a shock. To have trusted the secret of their kind to someone he'd known for so short a time?

"I know what you're thinking," Nils said. "But she is my fated mate and I wanted to ask her to join her life to mine. That meant she needed to know the truth in order to make an informed decision."

"What if she hadn't been able to handle it?"

"Desiree is not the woman she shows to the world. She is beautiful, yes, but so much more: strong, capable, intelligent, generous. Besides, unless I'm badly mistaken, her sister will be joining us, as well."

Anders chuckled. "Yes, well I fear the courting of *my* fated mate has not gone as well as yours. If this is what you want, then you not only have my permission, but my blessing. Perhaps I can find a way to use that to my advantage."

Nils shook his head. "I don't know about you, but with my fated mate so close, and not yet in my bed…"

"From the show she was giving you in Paris, I have to say that surprises me."

"Desiree needs to learn that she won't top from the bottom. I find a lot of females who play only at clubs are guilty of that. I have told her we will not consummate our relationship until we are bound together, and she has a ring to prove it."

"Then I suggest, old friend, we go for a very long run and perhaps a swim in the very cold ocean."

Both men removed their clothes and called forth their snow leopards. As the silvery swirl with the kaleidoscope of color and electrical shimmer receded, both men had become their alter egos. Normally, snow leopards were not found in Norway, but these were no normal snow leopards. They were larger, faster, more powerful, and more intelligent than their non-shifter kin.

The Nazis had encountered his ancestors and the Germans who survived those incidents had been discredited when they filed their reports. It was the account of the scarecrow confrontation—where a patrol had been impaled and stuffed with straw—and the continuing belief that something elusive and lethal and accompanied by snow leopards existed at Sabu, that ultimately led the Nazis to leave the stronghold alone.

This had allowed a small guerilla unit of shifters

to stalk, attack, and kill Nazis who wandered away from the relative safety of the town and provide cover and a distraction when the Shetland Bus needed to make a run. More than once, Sabu had been used as a safehouse and storage facility for the Allies.

Anders charged into Nils, bowling him over before whirling around and galloping toward the path that led to the beach. Though he might be bigger and stronger, Nils was a tad bit faster and quickly overtook his alpha, knocking him down and running past him. The two enormous cats ran, their white coats glistening in the moonlight, but not as a solid form. The black markings they bore served to provide a kind of camouflage in the moonlit night.

They wrestled in the sand with each other, testing one another's strength and fighting ability and displacing large amounts of sand. Finally, they both stormed into the water, racing each other to a barren rock that rose above the water's surface. Climbing up the side, they each shook, flinging water everywhere and ensuring neither got particularly dry. They sat silently, companionably, on the rock, looking back at Sabu.

Anders noticed Nils looking toward the room they had assigned to Desiree and wondered if his friend now regretted his decision. He admired Nils wanting to be honest and transparent with Desiree and knew if his friend trusted her to keep their secret, so could he. But Nils was right; she may as well know from the beginning that she would be truly submissive to her mate. It was the way of snow leopards—shifter or not.

Finally, they dove back into the ocean and swam to shore, each wallowing in the sand to remove as much water as he could from his coat before loping back to where they had left their clothes so they could shift and redress.

∼

When they first began removing their clothes, Gabriella thought she was in for a nice strip show, and the toned, muscular bodies that were revealed were impressive to say the least. As there was no one to see her as she gazed down from her window, she admired the way they were built. Anders was taller and a bit more muscular, but she was fairly sure Nils was just as deadly.

Anders was breathtakingly gorgeous—broad shouldered with a ripped chest and abs that formed an eight-pack. His thighs were powerful, and he had the most amazing hip notches that pointed straight to the promised land—a long, thick cock that seemed to defy gravity as it stood up, jutting out from his body. The moon chose that moment to shine directly down on them, casting enough light for her to see the light dusting of hair, perfectly placed on his chest and narrowing down as it ran down the centerline of his body, ending in a nest of curls surrounding the base of his staff.

She was just licking her lips and turning her attention to Nils when both were consumed by a silvery cloud of sparks and colors... *What the proverbial fuck?* As the blur began to clear, the place where once Anders and Nils had stood showed no trace of them. Instead, the settling of the color and light revealed two... snow leopards? Snow leopards were not indigenous to Norway, at least not since anyone had been recording history. The two creatures wrestled briefly with each other and then ran down the path to the beach.

What had happened to Anders and Nils? One minute they had been there, and the next two snow leopards had stood in their place. But where had the snow leopards been before the light show? It wasn't as if some magician was standing there with a cape, a wand, and a trick box where he could hide one pair until he could swap them out for the other. There was nowhere that she could see for the two men to be hiding.

Could it be? No, that was impossible. Human beings shifting into other creatures was the stuff of fairytales, fiction, and fantasy. And yet, it was the only answer available to her. Hadn't Sherlock Holmes once said something about when you eliminate everything else, you're left with the truth regardless of whether you wanted to believe it or not?

The primitive, lizard part of her brain told her to run, to get Desiree and to get the hell away from here —far, far away. The pair of snow leopards and then she and Desi composed a pair as well. It did not escape her notice that were this some sort of twisted fantasy, two predators plus two women whisked away with no one knowing where they were could equal something very, very bad. Was the meal they had eaten earlier been some kind of last meal for the condemned? Were she and her sister to become some sort of sacrifice in some pagan ritual where they were fed to these creatures?

Gabriella stood mesmerized, as if she were rooted to the floor, and watched as they disappeared out of sight, only to emerge on the beach. They wrestled with one another before plunging into the cold North Sea. Finally, she was able to force her attention away, grab her clothes and, after checking that the hallway was clear, rush down to her sister's room. Thank God, Desi hadn't locked her door—although she was sure that had more to do with Desi wanting more from Nils than a goodnight kiss than anything else.

"Gabi, what are you doing back here?" her sister said, sitting before the great fireplace that dominated one end of the room.

Gabriella snatched up her sister's clothing, tossing it at her as she began to pull her nightgown off and get dressed.

"Desi, we have to go. It isn't safe here."

"What are you talking about?"

"I can't tell you, but you have to trust me. Nils isn't the man you believe him to be." *In fact, he isn't a man at all!* "Hurry up. We need to get out of this place and get to somewhere we can steal a car. Do you remember where they told us they kept them?" Gabriella was pulling on her boots when she noticed Desi had yet to move. "What is wrong with you? Get dressed now."

"Gabi, everything is fine."

"Everything is *most definitely* not fine! For the love of God, Desi, get dressed. I don't know how long we have."

"How long for what?"

"Before Anders and his henchman return."

"What exactly do you think they're going to do to us?"

"You didn't see what I saw. I can't explain it. I can barely believe I saw it. But my guess is they're going to eat us."

Desiree smiled serenely. *Was she drugged? What the hell was wrong with her?*

"Do you think so?" Desi asked, hopefully. "Nils and I are negotiating about that. I maintain that 'consummate' is a synonym for 'fuck.' He maintains that any kind of sexual intimacy beyond kissing and maybe some light groping on his part is not going to happen until we're married. If I can't get him to change his mind, we're getting married tomorrow. But if you think I might be able to get at least some oral out of that stubborn man, we can actually plan a wedding... for a month from now. Honestly, Gabi, I haven't seen that thing he seems determined to keep in his pants. But I am determined to get hold of it and put it in a place it'll do both Nils and I some good."

Gabriella shook her sister. "Desi, get your mind out of the gutter and your libido under control. I just saw Anders and Nils morph into large cats—snow leopards, if I'm not mistaken."

"You aren't. It's pretty cool, isn't it?" What had happened to her sister? Gabriella slapped her sister across the face. "Ouch, Gabi. That hurt."

"Snap out of it. We have to go. Remember what he said about the Nazis being afraid to come up here? I think I know why. They must have some weird Viking cult and mean to sacrifice us at dawn..."

Desi laughed—downright laughed at her. "I'm fairly sure Anders wouldn't mind having you spread-eagled and tied down to something, but I promise the only thing he's interested in doing is seeing how many times he can make you come before he does."

Fuck it. Desi could come dressed in her nightgown. Gabriella wrapped her hand around Desi's wrist and jerked her to her feet. "Now, Desi."

Desi had no choice but to stumble after Gabriella who flung open the door only to run into Nils' chest. She looked around frantically for something to hit him with and found a heavy candlestick just inside the door. She released Desi's arm, took the candlestick in both hands and meant to swing it into his head.

"Gabriella," shouted Anders as he ran down the hallway toward them.

Fuck! They may be even in numbers but cat people or not, she and Desi were badly outmatched. Better to get back inside Desi's room. Maybe there was a secret way out or enough bedsheets to tie together to allow them to climb out of the window to the ground. Gabriella shoved Desi back into her room, but before she could get the door shut, Anders and Nils forced their way past the door to enter.

Thrusting Desi behind her, Gabriella brandished the heavy iron candlestick at Nils and Anders. If they rushed her, she and Desi didn't have a chance. Instead of advancing aggressively towards them, both Anders and Nils stopped just inside and Anders closed the door.

"What is the matter with your sister?" Nils asked Desi.

"Nothing is the matter with me, you mutant freak," snarled Gabriella.

Nils turned to Anders. "Your mate is in need of your steadying influence, Alpha."

"She saw the two of you shift," explained Desi quietly.

The soft and soothing tone of her sister's voice made Gabriella look away from Nils and Anders toward Desi, making her drop her guard. Before she could even think or breathe, Anders had wrapped his arm around her middle, lifting her off the ground as he removed the candlestick from her grasp.

He made a kind of purring noise that seemed to comfort her until she realized what it was and then it made her struggle with everything she had to get away from him. Nils must have done this to Desi. It was the only explanation that made sense.

Desi reached out to her, stroking Gabriella's cheek as she had when they were children and Gabriella had been frightened by something. "It's all right, Gabi. We aren't in any danger."

"You didn't see them," Gabriella said, trying to somehow cut through whatever drug Nils had given her sister to make Desi understand.

"I do understand, Gabi. It's you who doesn't. Understandable, as you weren't prepared. Anders fucked up."

"Desiree, you do not criticize our alpha," said Nils in a commanding, but not angry tone.

"I do, if he does," retorted Desi.

Nils shook his head. "Continue with that attitude, little one, and you will receive your first taste of my discipline without getting what I suspect it is you really want."

"Nils, she doesn't know our ways yet and she's right, I fucked up, for which I apologize. Gabriella was being difficult, and I thought to give her some time to get to know us. Not everyone is blessed with a fated mate who is so loving and accepting. By the way, Desiree, welcome to the clan."

"Thank you, Alpha," Desi answered.

Gabriella could feel her eyes widening in disbelief. Where was her smart ass, mouthy sister?

"Desi?" she said, incredulously.

"I promise it's okay, Gabi. They're snow leopard-shifters. The last of their kind. As you saw they can shift from their human form to their snow leopard form more easily than you or I can change our clothes. Aren't they the most beautiful creatures? And their fur is so soft." Desi's smile flashed across her face. "But I call foul—you got to see Nils naked, and I didn't get to see Anders."

"Desiree, my palm is starting to itch to spank that pretty bottom," warned Nils.

"Well, it's true. I don't think that's fair at all."

Gabriella shook her head. She'd been right—she and Desi had fallen down the rabbit hole.

CHAPTER 14

Anders continued to purr to her, holding her tight against his chest so she could feel the resonant rumbling. Much as she tried to ignore it, she couldn't and little-by-little, she felt her body relax into his and find comfort within his embrace.

"Good girl," he crooned before turning to Nils. "See to your mate and remember what we talked about."

"Yes, Alpha."

Anders used the arm not wrapped around her to curl up under the back of her knees and sweep her into his arms to cradle her next to his chest—that gorgeous, sculpted chest that sat above the eight-pack abs which led down to that amazing cock. *Stop it! It doesn't matter how ripped this guy is, he's a fucking mutant—some sort of weird were-leopard, were-snow leopard, were-cat... damnit, it doesn't matter.*

"Shh, Rella," he said soothingly as he walked down the hallway, past her door and into the enormous room at the end of the hallway.

"Don't call me that," she snarled. "And put me down."

"I will call you what I will, especially when we are alone. I prefer to keep you close," he said, sitting down in the large, overstuffed chair. "I'm sorry you had to see us shift without explanation. But at least you now know who and what we are. I can well imagine how frightening it was for you."

Gabriella continued squirming, trying to get away or at least get him to loosen his hold. It didn't work. In fact, he didn't even seem to notice. Finally, seeing the futility of her efforts, she settled down, allowing herself to rest against his chest.

"Well, it's not something you see every day, that's for damn sure. Is my sister safe with that freak?"

"Nils is not a freak, and you will not refer to any member of our clan in that derogatory manner."

"Look, just let my sister and me get out of here. Give me a single *krone* and we can say you engaged my services—that means I have to keep all of this confidential."

"True, but my engaging you would not keep Desiree from telling our secret if she chose to."

She nodded, considering his words. "No, but I can write up a quick non-disclosure agreement and that will cover her silence. There is no reason to kill us. In fact, if it would make you feel safer, we'll leave Europe all together."

"I have nothing to fear from you or your sister. Your sister would never betray us, and you, in turn, would never betray her."

"But my sister…"

"Is perfectly safe with her mate. You both understand the D/s lifestyle which is similar to the way we live. The only danger your sister is in is if she continues to try and lead Nils around by his cock, she is going to find herself nursing an uncomfortably red backside. Nils is my beta and helps me keep our she-cats in line."

"What do you mean by keep them in line?" she asked suspiciously, knowing that she wasn't about to hear anything to improve her opinion on the matter.

"She-cats are notoriously fractious creatures at the best of times. When they go into heat, they are all teeth and claws, becoming demanding, rude, belligerent, and downright nasty."

"So?"

"So, it falls to the alpha and beta of the clan to discipline the unmated she-cats when needed so that they are supported in being the best version of themselves. That duty falls to her mate if she is bonded, which is our version of being married, although over the centuries, the two rituals have combined and become one. As your sister is our beta's fated mate, her discipline will fall to him, now and for all time."

"What happens if they get divorced?"

He shook his head. "Snow leopards do not divorce. Desiree is Nils' fated mate and they will be bonded through this life and all those that come."

"That sounds a bit ominous."

"Only because you have yet to understand and accept our ways."

"Oh, I understand, all right. Your boy Nils means to force my sister to his bed and beat her whenever he gets it into his head to do so."

Anders shook his head. "Do not seek to bait me, Rella. It will do you no good. For one thing, it is incredibly hard to do, and for another, you won't like the consequences."

"How do you know that? Keep in mind that although we may know each other by reputation, you haven't known me very long. For all you know I might be a first-class pain slut."

"Highly unlikely. I would more easily believe that of your sister as she likes impact play. You on the other hand like being bound and suspended. You like the peace and quiet you can only find in subspace and the freedom to be found in restraint. Most likely you find it ironic, but you have learned it is true." He nuzzled her neck, nipping her earlobe. "I can teach you to fly so high, Rella." He chuckled. "I can also rig you up with a bright red tail."

"How do you know any of this?"

"I have made it my business to know as much as I can about you and your sister. You play at Dante's in Florence."

"How do you know that? Those records are confidential."

"The records, yes; the observations of the owner, no. Marco is a friend."

"Does he know about you?"

"That I am a gangster or that I am a shifter? It doesn't matter as he knows the answer to both. Trust me, no one plays at Dante's without Marco knowing who and what they are. He was reticent at first to discuss you with me, but he is something of a romantic at heart. When I told him you were my fated mate, he was only too happy to help."

"Remind me to cancel my membership at Dante's. And what the hell is a fated mate?"

"Your fated mate is the one who is the other half of your soul; the one who completes you. If you do not find each other in a lifetime, you are cursed to live only a half-life. While it is true of all shifters, it is especially true of alphas. Without our fated mate, the burden we carry can be unbearable. Only one's fated mate can give us solace and refuge."

Gabriella snorted. "What a load of romantic drivel. What makes you think I would even consent to play with you?"

"What makes you think I'm playing? I assure you

I am not. One of the chief differences between playing in a club and being a member of this clan is that here I, and I alone, deem what is fair and acceptable."

"I have to consent."

"Not in the world of shifters, although honorable men prefer if their partners agree to submit, but it isn't necessary. You are now subject to my authority, and rest assured I will keep you safe and happy. Although in some ways, this makes our business dealings easier. You will accept my assistance on my terms whether you like it or not."

"Does the idea of consent mean anything to you?"

He shrugged and shifted her on his lap to make her more comfortable. "Consent is preferred, but not necessary. Besides, once I have you beneath me, I will have you agreeing to whatever I want."

"I saw your cock. I'll give you that it's impressive, but I'm no simpering virgin so you and your almighty cock can go stuff yourselves."

He chuckled, seemingly truly amused with her. "That is precisely what I intend to do at some point— stuff my cock... up inside your sweet pussy."

Did he just threaten to rape me? Sure sounded like it. Gabriella drew back her fist and punched Anders in the nose, causing him to growl and release her so she could jump out of his lap. He felt his nose, growled again and then got up out of the chair, advancing on her as she ran for the door. She spotted a cast-iron candlestick very similar to the one in Desi's room and grabbed it. Gabriella turned, swung and caught him at the temple, dropping him to his knees before he crumpled to the ground.

She started to run from the room, but worried that she might have killed him. She approached him cautiously and felt for the pulse in his neck. Strong and steady. Good. She was out of here. Gabriella started down the hall to the room they were keeping Desi in. No, that was wrong, the look on Desi's face, her body posture, the way she spoke, all indicated she was right where she wanted to be. Desi was happier than Gabriella had seen her in months... years. Her sister seemed to know what she was doing, and despite her accusations to the contrary, Gabriella had no doubt her sister was safe with Nils.

Instead, Gabriella darted into her room, grabbed her duffle bag which should have her passport, credit cards, and cash. It seemed her brain was beginning to function again. It was still in the fight or flight mode, but at least she was thinking clearly enough to make flight to safety a definite possibility. She rushed down the main staircase, across the foyer, and out into the night.

Taking her bearings as she ran through the keep's main gate, she remembered having seen what might have been a boathouse down in the private cove. She wasn't sure, because at the time she was too busy admiring Anders' fine butt and his impressive package, but it made sense that they'd have some kind of watercraft down there.

Charging down the path, she glanced once over her shoulder. So far, so good—nobody was chasing her, but just as she looked, lights began to turn on in the castle, up along the walls and in the yard. Thankfully, it didn't look like they electrically illuminated the beach. She had made the first good decision since crossing paths with Anders Jensen.

Yes, there it was, a boathouse! *Please, God, let there be a boat or something in there she could use to get to safety.* If they asked her sister anything, she hoped Desi would remember her suggesting they needed to get to a car. She slowed down and crept up to the door of the boathouse and listened intently. Nothing. *Hallelujah!* No guards and a powerboat.

Gabriella flung her duffle onto the boat and moved up to the helm—she'd been on boats many times, but usually as a passenger. She was in luck; this one had a steering wheel and throttle that looked familiar. She untied the boat and pushed away from the dock. The rising tide lifted and moved it out toward the cove and the beckoning sea that lay beyond.

Starting up the engine, she moved out of the boathouse and into the open ocean. From atop the cliff, she heard a mighty roar. Not the loud, grunting roar of a lion, but a baritone kind of long sawing one.

Very distinctive. It sounded hoarse and was repeated several times.

She knew he had a plane. She hadn't seen a helicopter, but there had been a hangar. Gabriella would be surprised if he didn't have one. The most obvious route was to head for Denmark or maybe Germany, but if she knew that, so did he. She spotted an auto pilot and looked to see if there was any kind of history or frequent routes. Damn, Shetland was in there. That meant crossing the treacherous open waters of the North Sea, but that combined with how cold it would be made it the least desirable. Yep, the Shetland Islands it was.

Once she had engaged the autopilot, she ran below to see if there was anything that might help keep her warm in the open cockpit. Autopilot was fine for navigating, but she had no idea how it would work in close quarters or with someone in pursuit. She couldn't afford to stay below out of the wind and weather. She pulled on a heavy sweater and waterproof jacket, climbed back up to the navigation and steering section and wrapped a heavy blanket around her. Then she began to look for any kind of anti-theft system. Check. Disabled. Check. Next, find the transponders, which were a global tracking system. Found and turned off. Check.

Once past some tricky spots where it seemed imprudent to go at tremendous speed, she opened up the throttle and let the powerboat speed her away. She found a pair of binoculars below as well as a Keurig rigged for marine travel. At least the man—beast—how the hell did one refer to a creature like Anders? In any event, he was civilized, and as she sipped the dark French roast, warming her hands on the mug, she was grateful.

As she recalled from her research, the crossing would take anywhere from two to four days depending on the departure point and the roughness of the North Sea. Gabriella pushed the boat for as much speed as she could get, believing she was the most vulnerable on the open water in daylight. Luckily this area wasn't known for its bright, sunny skies.

She found extra petrol on board and monitored her fuel to ensure she never got below half a tank. Approximately three and a half days later, a beleaguered and exhausted Gabriella arrived in Scalloway on the Shetland Islands. She was able to find a place to tie up, promising the dock owner she would find lodging, get a nap and return. He wasn't happy about it, but a sufficient amount of cash allowed him to put his worries aside.

Gabriella had no intention of taking a nap. She needed to move fast if she was to have any hope of escaping Anders and whatever he had planned for her. She would need to find a way to contact Desi. She felt in her gut her sister was safe and that Nils returned Desi's feelings. Still, it hadn't felt right to leave her behind.

She found someone she could hire to drive her to the closest airport where she was able to purchase a prepaid cell phone. Once she was back either on the British mainland or on the Continent, she would contact Desi and once assured she was safe, she would ditch that phone too. Gabriella wanted more than anything in the world to go home to her little cottage on the outskirts of Nice, but that would be the first place Anders would look for her.

The safest place, if any place was safe from a man like Anders, would be New Orleans, but she wasn't all that crazy about bringing trouble home and she sure as hell didn't want to have to explain where Desi was. Assuming Desi was safe and happy, she could explain things to their family. Paris was the next best bet, but Anders knew the city and knew their hotel. On the other hand, Leclerc might be able to offer her protection.

She had all but promised Zofia Bendera she would recover her painting and she was convinced there was a very good chance it was located in Norway. He would never expect her to come back. Maybe she could base out of Denmark. There were plenty of small villages where she might be able to rent something. She could tell them she was doing research and writing a novel. But how to get there? While she sat in the airport, a plan came to mind—partly because the first flight out was to London. She would fly to London and take the high-speed train to Callais where she'd buy a vehicle of some sort and then make her way to Denmark.

She would find the cache of Nazi stolen artwork and return all of it, including the Durer drawing Anders had coveted, and then figure out her next move. If she could pull this off, her reputation would be such that Anders wouldn't dare to touch her.

The flight to London went smoothly—at least it wasn't rough enough to wake her from a dead sleep. Once she was on the high-speed train to Callais, she called Desi's phone.

"Gabriella? Is it you? Please let it be you!"

Her sister sounded frantic. Oh God, had she made the wrong choice? Was Desi in danger? If so, trying to keep this low key was out, her next call would be to Leclerc and then to Interpol. If Anders had allowed her sister to be harmed in any way, she would bring a shitshow of police to his door.

"Desi, I'm sorry. I thought you wanted to be there?"

"Oh, I do. But you're okay, right?"

"I am. At least so far."

"So far?"

"You know Desi, it's kind of a lot. I wanted to make sure you were okay."

"Never better. Nils has been so sweet to me. He even relented on the whole no consummating the relationship... well, we haven't fucked yet, but I have gotten my hands and mouth on his magnificent cock. It's yummy and I want him to fuck me so badly. If he is half as talented with his dick as he is with his mouth, it's going to be amazing."

Gabriella started to laugh. Desi was fine.

"Anders is pissed, and I mean pissed. Nils said he's never seen him so agitated. He says it's because he really believes that bullet was meant for you. I think it's because he has feelings for you. Do you know snow leopards have fated mates? Kind of like a soulmate, but even more intense. The males know them instantly; I think your Anders believes you to be his. He wants you back and he's dispersed men all over Europe to find you. Nils and I are getting married in six weeks and then I'll get to be made into a snow leopard."

Gabriella hadn't been paying much attention to Desi's rambling; she'd just been happy to hear her voice and know her sister was happy. Did Desi just say she would become a snow leopard?

"Desi? What do you mean you'll become a snow leopard? Like you won't be human?"

"Well, I'll be human part of the time. And part of the time I'll be a snow leopard. Want to know the best part? I'll be able to eat anything and not gain weight. Isn't that a hoot? After all these years of starving myself, I can indulge, and the chef here is amazing. Wait!"

Again, Gabriella had allowed her attention to lapse, but the note of concern in Desi's voice made her sit up and pay attention.

"Gabriella," said Nils in his dominant, calm voice. "Where are you? Anders is beside himself. You will tell me at once where you are."

"I wouldn't hold my breath waiting for that. You take good care of my sister and tell Anders to find someone else. I'm not interested in the job of fated mate to a gangster. Your secret is safe with me as long as I know my sister is safe and happy. Tell Desi I love her."

Gabriella ended the call, destroyed the SIM card and battery, and then disposed of both as well as the phone itself in three separate trash cans on separate cars. She barely had time to complete her task when the train pulled into Calais. Gabriella stepped out into the foggy, misty morning and hailed a cab.

Turned out she picked the right guy. A mechanic friend of his had taken the title in lieu of payment for work done on a vehicle. A quick stop at the local branch of her bank and she had a good amount of cash and the title to a two-year-old, cinnamon-colored Peugeot 2008. The color was gorgeous, but she would have preferred black to blend in, but nevertheless the thing was in great shape, had low miles, and all the bells and whistles, including a panoramic sunroof. She'd thought about something smaller, but decided she needed to be comfy, have room for whatever she wanted to carry and power to burn. Anders might be able to track her to Calais, but she had spent less than two hours in the city before she was well away and headed back to the lion's—or in this case, the snow leopard's—territory.

CHAPTER 15

***S**kjult Fjord*
  Kattegat, Norway
Present Day

Gabriella took a deep breath, trying to catch some air. 'Hidden Fjord' was right. This thing had been damn hard to find. And then there had been the whole confusion about whether or not Kattegat even existed and if it did was it a town? Was it even in Norway? All of her research had been contradictory. She had absolutely no hard evidence that such a place as Kattegat or Skjult Fjord even existed.

One night when she was no more than five, Gabriella had gone into the attic in her family's home on a dark and stormy night and discovered a trunk that had once belonged to her great-grandmother. It had been riffled through over the years, but at the bottom, in a secret compartment, Gabriella had found the real treasure—her great-grandmother's diaries. In them, she spoke of meeting with members of the Polish Underground, one of whom was a young woman whose ancestor's portrait had been painted by Leon Wyczółkowski. The portrait had been loaned to the Museum of Warsaw and had disappeared from the museum when the Nazis had invaded. It was an evocative, bordering on erotic, portrait; the woman had feared it would never be returned to the family.

Her great-grandmother had tried to find out what had happened to her friend after she'd been captured, as well as to the rest of her family, and to the portrait. The family had been caught up in the burning of the Warsaw Ghetto in 1943. Some of them had survived being captured only to be shipped off and killed in one of the Nazi concentration camps. The painting, spirited away by the Nazis, had disappeared and was never seen or heard of again.

Gabriella's imagination had been captured by the diaries. Armed with her advanced degrees, she had followed her sister to France, but instead of Paris, Gabriella had set up shop in Nice. It boasted a large airport which made it easier to travel and follow her passion for representing ex-patriated clients who were still trying to recover artwork and other treasures stolen by the Nazis.

As she reached the top of the fjord and looked

down its length she sighed. "Why couldn't the damn Nazis just have marked it with a big X. It would make it so much easier to find."

Gabriella was convinced the cache of Nazi treasures her great-grandmother had alluded to in her diaries was here somewhere in Skjult Fjord.

All she had to do now was find it… well, that and make sure Anders Jensen, the head of the Valhalla Syndicate, didn't find her first.

~

Anders paced back and forth in his study, grumbling and growling as he checked his mobile phone again. Why hadn't they called? Why hadn't he gone instead?

"Anders if it was her, they'll pick up her trail and find her," Nils calmly assured him.

"Not so far they haven't," he growled, "How many times have I thought to have her home at Sabu only for her to slip through my fingers again?"

There was a knock on the door and Desiree stuck her head in. Anders had hoped, even knowing it was a longshot, that Gabriella might return to Sabu for her sister's wedding and bonding ceremony to Nils. Desiree's family had been here—her parents and her brother Marc, as well as cousins and friends. The castle had been filled to overflowing. Anders had told Desiree that if her sister wished to attend the wedding, he would allow her to come and go. Naturally, that was a lie. It was one of the reasons he'd insisted that the wedding be held at Sabu. If Gabriella had attended, he would have sprung his trap and ensured she remained at his side and in his bed.

Anders had no doubt that both Gabriella and Desiree, and perhaps even Nils, would protest his underhanded treatment. But Anders didn't care. Noble and truthful had cost him this time with his fated mate. Had he not underestimated her, they would have most likely been through whatever settling-in period Gabriella might need.

Desiree and Gabriella kept in touch. Gabriella would call Desiree and talk for no more than twenty minutes and then would hang up, destroying and disposing of the phone as soon as the call ended. He had assured Desiree that he would not try to trace the call, but his fated mate had not believed his assurances. At least Gabriella kept in touch with Desiree, providing him with a way to know she was safe. After a while, he stopped trying to trace the source of the call, although he had listened in.

At first, he had told himself it was to ensure she was safe, then to see if he could pick up any clues as to her whereabouts, but finally he had been forced to admit that it was because he missed the sound of her voice—especially when she laughed. Desiree's laugh was like champagne, bubbling in the sunshine; Gabriella's a good whiskey—complex and smokey.

"I'm taking it we've had no word?" asked Desiree,

taking Nils up on his invitation to sit in his lap.

Desiree could most often be found either curled in Nils' lap or at his feet. She had taken on a great many of the duties that should have been done by mate to the alpha, but Anders' mate was off running around, putting herself in danger and causing him no end of frustration and worry. He hadn't done without a woman since he'd discovered the ecstasy to be found in stroking a woman's pussy. But he could not find it within himself to touch another. He would have Gabriella or no other—and he didn't mean to continue to do without.

He was still not certain who had taken a shot at Gabriella back in Paris, but he was convinced she had been the target. Joshua Knight of the Tiamat Syndicate in England had called to advise him that they had captured an assassin working for the bratva and had discovered a list of names—Gabriella's name had been on it. Before he could be questioned properly, the man had wrestled a gun away from one of the guards and put a bullet in his own brain. The bratva did not tolerate failure and by killing himself, he had most likely spared his family.

"None. They think she may have crossed over into Norway," said Nils, nuzzling his mate.

"At least she's closer," offered Desiree as comfort. "When she calls next do you want me to tell her about the assassin in England?"

Anders nodded. "Yes. If she will not allow me to

keep her safe, I don't want her out there operating blindly. Ask her again if she won't at least speak to me."

"I do, Alpha, every time."

Anders smiled at Desiree. "I know you do. You're a good girl and Nils is lucky to have you."

"So she tells me," teased Nils.

"She just didn't understand," started Desiree.

"I know," said Anders. "As you said, I fucked up."

Desiree groaned and rolled her eyes before batting them at Nils. "Is he ever going to let me live that down?"

Nils chuckled. "Probably not. After all, you are so perfect, he has nothing else to tease you about."

"I know, but sometimes I think he believes it."

Anders smiled at her, knowing the shape of his lips didn't match the sadness in his eyes. "Sometimes, you're right." His mobile buzzed and he answered, putting it on speaker, "Yah?"

"We believe she crossed over from Denmark. This time coming into Norway through Kristansand. We were able to confirm that about ten days ago, she met with someone in Berlin, then flew to Oslo to speak with someone there before going off the grid again. I know you're angry with her and worried for her, but she's got some mad hiding skills."

Anders laughed. His man was right. It was the only thing that allowed him to get any sleep at all. Both Desiree and Nils were now on him about his lack of sleep. They were right, he was exhausted. Once he had Gabriella home, safe in his arms with a bright red tail from his discipline, he'd wrap her up in his arms and sleep for a week. Well, that wasn't true, he'd have her again, and again, and again. He would revel in the sound of hearing her yowl as his barbs scored her inner walls and he took the nape of her neck in a claiming bite. Then, and only then, would he allow himself the luxury of sleep.

"Any idea where she's headed?" asked Anders.

"We think she may be headed for the fjords up above Sabu."

Anders hit the switch that lowered his electronic white board on which he'd been tracking her movements and any clues she might have come across. Twice they had tried to bait her to see if they couldn't pick her up, but she had outfoxed them both times. He was frustrated, angry, worried, and proud. Given the number of police agencies, private security and friends he had looking for her, she had managed to elude them.

"Keep on her if you can. If you confirm she's made her way back here, we can use our men to cover the area."

"Yes, Alpha. We will do our best."

"I know you will. As you say, she is very, very good at this." He ended the call and looked at Nils. "Send our people into Bergen. Get a tap on Zofia Bendera and her husband if you can—cars, phones, house, the lot of it. If Gabriella is in the area, I want to know if she tries to contact them."

"I wish we could entice her husband to join our cause," said Nils.

Anders laughed. "Never happen. The man's a major pain in the ass, but loyal, and damn good at what he does."

"Yah, things would be easier if we could get him to join those that work with and for us."

Desiree looked at her mate. "You sound like you admire him."

Anders nodded. "He does. So do I. The man is incorruptible. I mean if I held a gun to his wife's head, he'd do whatever I wanted, but short of threatening her or their children…"

"Which you would never do," said Desiree with confidence.

"No. I wouldn't. If I was forced to do something to him, it would be to him and him alone and then I would ensure his family was cared for."

"Gabriella doesn't understand that. She's seen too many gangster movies," Desiree assured him.

"I know. I disregarded my instincts and thought to woo her. I should have just claimed what was mine and dealt with her temper."

"You might have found that far more difficult to deal with than you imagine," said Desiree.

Anders chuckled. "No doubt. But I thought I'd

have more time. I know it was fast, but Nils managed to convince you…"

"But I'm easy and Gabriella is not. She has always followed her head. I always followed my heart." Nils growled quietly; Desiree rolled her eyes. "I'm not saying I'm not smart. I'm merely saying I tend to lead with my emotions, followed by my intelligence. Gabriella is just the opposite."

"I'm sorry my lack of action cost you her presence at your bonding ceremony."

"It's all right. I gave her your message; she chose not to believe. Besides, Nils says when she comes back, and you let her out of seclusion, we can have a huge party to celebrate."

Anders smiled. "Indeed, we shall."

"Dagmar wanted me to remind you two that dinner is at six. You've both been late the past few nights."

"You and Dagmar would do well to remember that it is not your place to scold your alpha," admonished Nils.

"Maybe, but it upsets the clan and brings home the reminder that our alpha's mate is missing and in danger," said Desiree in a quiet, submissive voice.

Would he ever hear Gabriella defer to him that way? Did he really care? No, what he wanted was her here at Sabu, safe in his arms. Desiree rose gracefully from her mate's lap and left them in the study.

"She isn't wrong, you know," offered Nils.

"I know. I think I'll go for a short run. Maybe I can burn off some of this frustrated sexual energy."

"A dip in the cold ocean wouldn't go amiss."

Anders stopped at the door. "We have to find her Nils. I have a feeling that whoever is after her is closing in."

"We're doing everything we can, Anders. It doesn't help that your mate is as clever as you."

Anders strode back to the changing area that was set up at the back of the keep. Removing his clothes, he felt his other half, perhaps his better half, come charging to the fore as a swirl of shimmering silvery sparks, bolts of bright white energy, and an array of swirling colors surrounded him. When it had dissipated, he was man no longer.

Bounding out the door, he ran to the promontory. It was the last place he had seen her. As he had that night, he roared into the wind in anger and anguish. She had run from him and never looked back. He believed Desiree when she told him that his mate longed for him as he did for her, and that if they could just bring her home, all would be well.

He charged down to the beach and galloped along the shore, first on the hard-packed sand, then in the frigid waters of the North Sea and then back up onto the loose sand. The beach had always been a place the clan came to run and play, hidden from the rest of the world, but he could no longer abide sharing it with anyone else. He would run the cliffs and hills with those in his clan and watch over them from the precipice, but when they ventured down to the sands, he would remain atop the cliff and keep watch—whether it was over them or for her, he didn't know.

The different textures of sand felt good beneath his feet, and he allowed himself to enjoy the freedom and joy that it was to be his snow leopard. He was looking out to sea, roaring long and low in a kind of quiet desperation when he felt something hit his flank. His snow leopard took control and whirled to growl and challenge whoever had dared attack him.

The human within looked to the site of his discomfort. It was a damn tranquilizer dart. They kept them for emergencies. Their alpha being bereft did not rise to the level of emergency. He looked up to the top of the cliff to see who dared to have shot him.

Desiree. He should have known it. She shared her sister's dogmatic approach to getting her way. Apparently, she had decided he needed to rest, so rest he would, whether he liked it or not. Damn, that thing was painful. He tried reaching around to grab it in his teeth to pull it out. When that didn't work, he tried to shift, but didn't have the resources to do so.

Anders began to feel woozy, and his hind end seemed to have a mind of its own. It refused to follow where his front end was leading, which was back up to the castle to inform his beta that he expected Nils to blister her backside.

He could feel his back legs tremble and collapse, and no matter how hard he tried, he could not get them under control in order to allow him to get back on his feet. Two men followed her down the path with a litter. He growled and gnashed his teeth at her.

"I know; I know," she soothed. "You want Nils to make sure I can't sit for a week; it is unseemly for the mate of the beta to shoot the alpha in the ass with a tranquilizer dart. Trust me, he was having similar thoughts when I dropped him. You don't sleep; he doesn't sleep."

Anders collapsed on the sand and Desiree came to raise his head out of it and continued. "You think he goes to bed when he enters our chambers, but you're wrong. He comes in, makes mad, passionate love to me and then leaves to go stand guard over you. Well, I'm not having it. We will find her, and we will bring her home. And when my sister gets here—notice I said when, not if—I'm going to have words with her about this bullshit and how put upon I've been."

The last she said with her trademark sassiness that never failed to make him and Nils laugh at her, which was her intention. He made a chuffing noise, which was a snow leopard's way of chuckling.

"I love you too, Anders," she said, kissing his head as the men moved him onto the litter and then followed her back up the path to the castle.

She was right—they would find Gabriella, they would bring her home, and he would claim his mate with all the primal, feral energy it took to get the job done once and for all. And then, she would never leave his side again.

CHAPTER 16

Gabriella trudged along a path that only mountain goats were meant to tread… and she wasn't too sure about them. She had her walking stick, her compass, her map and her backpack. Her legs were beginning to feel like trembling lead weights which seemed somewhat incongruous to her, but was what she felt, nonetheless.

It had been a long, hard six months and the cost to her had been immeasurable. She had missed Desi's bonding ceremony. Her parents were furious; Marc was suspicious. Desi had assured her numerous times that Anders was willing to give her a free pass in and out of Bergen so that she could be there. She trusted that Desi was sincere and that she believed, but Gabriella didn't believe him at all.

He'd tried to trick her in order to trap her twice

and there had been numerous other close calls. Several times she was sure she was being followed but could never quite figure out who it was or where they were. Desi was now convinced that Anders was right, and Gabriella was in danger. At first, she had been furious that Anders wanted to frighten her sister that way, but little by little Gabriella had come to believe that if nothing else, Anders believed he was right, but who would want to kill her?

Anders had suggested both the bratva and the Odessa had good reason to kill her. She didn't buy the bratva—neither she, nor any member of her family had run afoul of them. The Odessa might have cause, especially as she grew closer and closer to finding the cache of treasure stolen by the Nazis. Many of the elite officers had fled Germany when it became clear that Hitler's madness would not save them.

Most had made use of what had been termed the 'ratlines'—the main two routes being Germany to Spain to Argentina, or alternately Germany to Rome to Genoa, and then to South America. But there had been a third 'ratline' that ran from Germany to Oslo to Bergen, and then to the United Kingdom or Ireland. It was rumored that the haul taken from the University of Warsaw and the Warsaw Museum had been divided into thirds. One cache had been discovered; bits and pieces of a second had begun to make their way out of their hiding places. But the main cache—the one containing the most valuable pieces, had been diverted North and been hidden somewhere in the fjords.

At least those traveling the various 'ratlines' had known some of the uncertainty, if not terror, they had inflicted on their victims. Some of those who had thought themselves relatively safe once onboard a Norwegian boat headed west discovered mid-journey that they were not safe at all. Those operating the boats had tossed their Nazi passengers into the North Sea to die from hypothermia and drowning—neither a pleasant way to go—while watching them slip beneath the waves.

When asked if he believed their execution of the German officers to be cruel, one man had replied, "No. Cruel would have been to bring them back on the boat, gotten them warm and comfortable… and then thrown them overboard again." Everything Gabriella had learned made her tend to agree with the man's assessment. Shaking her head to clear it of such morbid and ghastly thoughts and visions, she trudged on.

Just as she picked her way down a particularly difficult hilly terrain, two men stepped out from behind rocks with guns. She might have worried they were Anders' men, as she was closer to Sabu than she had dared to go in the past six months, but the guns were a sure-fire sign these were not his people. She turned to flee, which was relatively stupid as they had guns and a clear field of fire. Even if she'd been able to make it back up the hill, two men she thought she had spotted before crested the rise above and began to make their way down.

She was majorly fucked. This was not the first time she had envied her sister's new ability to shift into a snow leopard and bound away. Well, nothing to do but brazen it out and hope they made a mistake and left her an opening.

"Gentlemen, may I help you?"

"*Nein, Fräulein.*"

Okay; that one at least was German or at least he spoke German like a native.

"At last, we have you where we want you," said one of the others in an accent she was fairly sure was Russian.

Maybe Anders had been half right—it wasn't the bratva or the Odessa, it was both.

"This is interesting. I was told as a rule Odessa and bratva hate each other," she said, trying to provoke a reaction. If she was going to die, she really wanted to know why.

"Normally, this is true, but you have become a prize to several interested parties among both groups. What is it they want from you?"

"You tell me and we'll both know," she said, pleasantly.

Not for the first time, she thought her decision not

to even speak with Anders might have been a mistake. Okay, clearly a mistake, as she was fairly certain if she had stayed with Anders, she wouldn't be facing the real possibility of her own demise. As the four men began to stalk her slowly, she had time to think of several things she wished she'd done differently. If nothing else, she really wished she'd had sex with Anders. Desiree described sex with Nils as nothing short of mind blowing.

"Oh my God, Gabi… well, you saw how well hung he was, and the man knows how to use what his mama gave him. He makes this purring noise and sometimes it's just really soothing and sometimes it's the most arousing sound. When he's stroking inside me, he makes this amazing growling noise. Gives me shivers just to think of it," Desi said with enormous enthusiasm.

The term TMI had never occurred to Desi.

"So, are you a snow leopard now?"

"Only when I want to be. It's pretty amazing, it feels like the lightest setting of a violet wand going all over your body and there's lots of lights and silvery sparkles and suddenly you look down and you're a snow leopard. You can hear her thoughts, but you're always in control. And you experience everything through her senses, and yet you know you're human."

"Okay, I have to say that doesn't sound too bad," said Gabriella, thoughtfully.

"It's not. And it feels the same when you go back

to human form. If you don't take your clothes off, they just disintegrate, but interestingly jewelry doesn't, but you can't see it on the snow leopard. I kind of freaked the first time because I thought I'd lost my ring. I like to tease Nils and change back when I don't have any clothes close by."

Gabriella laughed. "Of course, you do. How do they do it? Is it like they give you an injection?"

"Hmm. I can't decide if that would be better or worse. Probably wouldn't hurt as much but wouldn't be as much fun either. The transition itself is a breeze. It's the claiming bite that's a bitch. It's the bite that triggers the transition, or as they call it, the Gift."

"What do you mean bite? Like a love nip?"

"No, they do it when they're fucking you from behind. Their fangs elongate and they take hold of your neck and bite down. After that, it's intense but amazing."

"You sound so happy, Desi," Gabriella said, a part of her a bit envious.

"I am. You could be too, Gabi. Anders loves you…"

Gabriella snorted.

"He does. He hasn't touched another woman… I mean not so much as looked at one since you left. Considering the over-the-top libido Nils said he used to have, and that my sources said my mate shared as well, that's saying a lot.

"Well, I don't love him."

"That's such bullshit, Gabi. I saw the way you looked at him. Lie to me if you like, but for heaven's sake, don't lie to yourself. Just think about it. He's convinced you're his fated mate. Nils said he'll never take another."

"I'm glad it makes you happy, Desi; really, I am."

"Fine, but when he catches up with you, and he will, don't blame me if he welts your ass before he claims you."

"You almost sound like you want him to."

"Well, I don't want him to welt your ass, although, frankly, I'm not sure you don't deserve it, but I do wish you had him to hold you at night and to make love to you. You should have seen mama. She was pissy because we wanted to be married here in Norway at Sabu. I'm not sure what she was thinking, but when she saw it was a castle, she was pretty impressed. For the record, she thinks you're just being stubborn."

"Oh, that's nice, I'm trying to reunite people with things that were stolen by the Nazis and my family is talking trash about me," Gabriella said laughing.

"Well, daddy was kind of on Marc's side. You should call him if you can; he's worried about you. But daddy saw that chess set in Anders' office, and he gave it to him. Just had it boxed up and gave it to him. Daddy said the thing is worth about a hundred grand."

"Desi, I know what you said about them

promising not to try and trace these calls, but I have to go."

"Anders gave me his word, and Nils said that man never breaks his word."

"He's still a gangster, Desi."

"Yeah, but a nice gangster."

Gabriella laughed again. She missed her big sister. "I don't even want to know what you mean by that. I love you Desi."

"I love you too, Gabi. I miss you. Come home."

Desi ended every single phone conversation the same way. 'I love you. I miss you. Come home." But Gabriella's home wasn't Sabu Stronghold. As she refocused on the men coming toward her, she wondered if perhaps it could have been and was sad that she would never see Desi again and never know if Anders was the lover Desi thought he would be.

"You are going to tell us everything you know," said the man with the thick Russian accent. "You know where the treasure is, and you will tell us."

"Now, why on earth would I do that? If I tell you, you'll just kill me, which doesn't seem like a very good deal for me. How about you offer me the finder's fee?"

"Yah, we could do that," said the German.

"You dolt. She wants to reunite the art with its previous owners who were too stupid to keep it," said the Russian, the last bit was cut off as Gabriella's hand cracked across his cheek.

"You call me what you want. You do whatever you need to do, but you will not insult in any way those whose lives were destroyed by the Nazis," said Gabriella. If she was going to die, she was going to do it on two feet, standing up for something she believed in.

Suddenly four red dots appeared, one on the forehead of each of her would be assailants. Then a split second after both she and they noticed them and recognized them for what they were, four shots rang out in unison—the sound deafening as it echoed along the high walls of the fjord. Instinctively, Gabriella dropped to her knees, the blood from the fatal gunshots in the men's heads, soaking the earth and making lazy rivulets in the dirt as it wound its way around her.

She wasn't certain how long she huddled like that, but suddenly two arms crushed her in their embrace as he lifted her from the muck and the mire.

"Gabriella, thank God you're safe. Thank God we got here in time," said Anders before his mouth came down on hers with sensual purpose, his tongue sweeping through her mouth.

It occurred to her that this was the first time he'd ever kissed her. Normally, Gabriella didn't like kissing, it was usually just wet and awkward. This might be wet, but there was nothing awkward in the way his lips claimed hers and demanded her response. When he lifted his head, she saw everything—the stark fear and anger that he'd almost lost her, and the relief that they had arrived in time. She still lived and breathed and had become wildly aroused. Her mouth wasn't the only thing that was wet.

Gabriella knew she ought to push him away… create some distance between them. But she couldn't do it. For one thing, he'd just saved her life. For another, she'd really liked kissing him and wouldn't mind kissing him not just again, but more. And the last thing was, having his arms wrapped around her had made her feel safe for the first time in a long time, maybe even longer than before she left Sabu.

"Thank you seems a bit inadequate. I do believe these guys meant to kill me."

"Inadequate doesn't even begin to cover it," he said, fisting her hair, tugging her head back and crushing his mouth against hers once again.

Anders was holding her close enough and tight enough that she could feel the hard line of his erection, throbbing against her belly as the Viking came to the fore, his mouth telling her everything she'd ever need to know about pillaging and plundering. She suddenly understood why Desi had been so desperate to get Nils naked and inside her. Gabriella felt the same way. She wasn't sure she'd even offer a protest if he stripped her naked and fell on her, parting her thighs with his and shoving every inch of his hard cock deep inside her.

Instead of resisting, much less fighting, Gabriella leaned into his strength and muscle. It felt like heaven to sag into him, to give over and let him get them out of here.

"Hagen, Dahl dispose of the bodies. Berg, Eriksen, you're with me. Let's get Gabriella back to Sabu and then you can come back and help Dahl and Hagen. Come on, Gabriella, we're going home. As soon as we're airborne, I want you to call your sister. We may only be thirty minutes from Sabu, but I want her to know you're safe as soon as possible."

"And am I? Safe?"

"From the outside world? Absolutely. I will keep you safe. From me? That depends entirely on how you define that word."

"I know I should be grateful," she said, trying to pull away.

"I don't have the time or the inclination to put up with any more of your bullshit."

Anders turned back to her, scooping her up and tossing her over his shoulder. When she tried to straighten up, he smacked her ass and not in a friendly, sexy kind of way. No, this was in an 'obey me or else' kind of way. When she squirmed around, he smacked her again.

"Knock it off, Gabriella or I swear I'll bare your backside and give you the first of what I'm pretty sure will be numerous and memorable spankings."

Something about his tone of voice let her know

that this was not an idle threat and there was a part of him that was looking forward to it.

Gabriella subsided.

CHAPTER 17

Anders settled her into the back seat of the helicopter, between himself and the man he'd called Berg, who fitted her with a headset. Silently the rotors of the chopper turned in lazy circles. Then with a deftness of skill she'd rarely seen, Eriksen put the helicopter in motion. She was surprised when the chopper began to move forward and lift off and clutched Anders' arm.

"It's all right, Gabriella. Eriksen is very good at his job," soothed Anders.

"I'm fine in helicopters. In fact, I love them. It just caught me by surprise because it didn't sound loud enough. Come to think of it, I didn't hear it come in when you came to save me."

Anders chuckled. "That's because it has stealth capability."

"I thought only the military had stealth copters."

"And they're also supposed to be the only ones with armor plating and weaponry, but as you can see for yourself, that isn't the case."

"Is it legal?" she asked.

"No, but as you like to point out ad nauseam, I'm a gangster. Illegal doesn't really bother me. Call your sister. She's waiting."

He tapped one of the buttons on the outside of the ear cups and she could hear the sound of a ringtone.

"Gabi?" cried Desi.

"Yeah, Desi, I'm with Anders. We're safe. Everyone with him is fine, not a mark on them. The bad guys are all dead."

"Shit! Shit! Shit! Ouch! Sorry, if the bad guys are all dead it means they barely got there in time. Anders wanted at least one of them alive. And the ouch was because Nils doesn't like it when I use bad language. But you're okay?"

"Uhm, a little shaken up, but not bad, all things considered. We should be there in just a bit."

Anders tapped her mic, turning it off and turning on his own. She could still hear everything; she just couldn't say anything.

"Desiree, put Nils on the phone," barked Anders.

"Alpha? Our people are fine?"

"As my mate told her sister. Good guys win, bad guys are dead."

"Damn."

Anders chuckled in a grim tone. "Tell me about it. You are going to need to deal with your mate and the clan. I am taking Gabriella into seclusion for the next few days."

"Do you want me to have an officiant standing by?"

"At some point… but there are things Gabriella and I need to settle before then."

Gabriella could feel her eyes widening in alarm and she really didn't like the cheeky look on Berg and Eriksen's faces. Anders disconnected the call and turned her mic back on.

"Careful how you speak to me, mate. You have a lot to make up for."

"I don't recall agreeing to marry you," she said, not sure whether to be really pissed off or think the whole thing was incredibly funny.

"That's because I didn't ask you. The last time you were at Sabu, I wanted to play the attentive lover to give you time to get to know and understand us. I won't make that mistake this time. I mean to take you to mate and claim you as mine."

"I have no choice in the matter?"

"None whatsoever. Technically, that's not true. You can apologize to me for the hell you've caused everyone and behave yourself…"

"We both know that doesn't sound a lot like me," she snarked.

"Then you can choose the other option, which is

to have me put you face down over my knee, welt your pretty backside and be forced to your knees in tears while an officiant speaks the legal bullshit." He looked at his watch. "You have approximately ten minutes to decide."

When they landed in the bailey of the castle, she said as he helped her out, "I thought you didn't allow motorized vehicles inside the estate's walls."

"I'm making a special exception for you," he growled. "Berg and Eriksen need to get back to our people in the fjord and finish cleaning up the mess you made."

"Me?" she protested. "You're the one who shot them and made them bleed all over the place."

"And had you been home by my side where you belong, that wouldn't have been necessary."

"Well, you can't just haul me into your bedchamber, fuck me from behind, bite my neck and claim me as yours."

"You couldn't be more wrong," he said in a sinister tone. "Try not to cause your sister any more heartache or worry, will you?"

Before she could protest, tell him he was being unfair, or call him an asshole, he dragged her body into his, his mouth slamming down on hers to shut her up. Heat and desire flooded her system, blooming and washing over her like a tsunami hitting the beach. He fisted her hair, wrapping her long red locks around it and angling her head where he wanted—where it suited him.

Gabriella heard her sister exclaim as Anders locked his body against hers, forcing her to rest her body along his as he continued to kiss her with seduction and force. She could feel both in equal measure. He backed off, withdrawing his tongue to trace along the seam of her lips, before plunging back in like an invading army. Everything but Anders began to fade away until all but him and her burgeoning feelings for him were on soft focus.

She moaned as she sagged against him, her knees beginning to buckle and her toes curling. No two ways about it, Anders Jensen knew how to kiss. In fact, he took kissing to a whole other level. But it wasn't just his dominance that was her undoing, it was the overwhelming feeling of seduction. His tongue slid into her mouth, dancing with hers and inviting her to play. The fist in her hair tightened and she could feel her scalp tingling as he ramped up her arousal. Gabriella had to keep her wits about her, or she was going to start humping the hard thigh he had wedged between hers.

Suddenly her bra was really uncomfortable—the too tight, too scratchy material irritating her nipples as they pebbled and pushed against the seam of the lace. Passion bloomed, saturating her system and turning her into a puddle of need.

Releasing the arm that held her tight against his

body, he allowed that hand to trace the curve of her spine before cupping her ass and pulling it even closer, ensuring her mons was pressed tight up against his groin and the throbbing evidence of his own need filtered through her lust-addled brain. He kneaded and fondled her ass and she rubbed herself against him like an alley cat—or she supposed in this instance, a snow leopard—in heat.

What had her sister said about him biting her? Gabriella wound her arms around him, rising up on her tiptoes to stretch along his tall, muscular body. God, was this what Desi had experienced that first night with Nils? No wonder she'd fallen so hard. This wasn't just seduction; this was dominance in its purest form and every bit of her responded to it and him. He wanted to bite her neck? Fine. He wanted to blister her ass? Again, fine. Wanted to fuck her right here in the bailey with his entire clan watching and cheering him on? That too, was perfectly acceptable. In fact, she thought that last option sounded fine indeed.

Scooping her up in his arms and cradling her to his chest as if her weight was nothing, Anders headed into the keep and up the main staircase, striding down the hall until they reached his bedchamber. She had a sudden memory of having clocked him with a heavy candlestick.

"Does it mitigate anything that I came back to make sure you were breathing, and your pulse was strong and steady?" she asked hopefully. Gabriella was pretty damn sure that by the time the shouting was over she was going to have a very well-spanked ass and be sore in places she'd never been sore before.

"Need I remind you if you hadn't swung an iron candlestick into my skull, there wouldn't have been any doubt that I was unharmed?"

"Okay, but you have to admit, it's not normal to see someone change from human to snow leopard."

"Depends on where you live. Here at Sabu, it is not at all unusual."

Okay, this wasn't going the way she'd hoped. He shouldered open the door and kicked it closed behind him. Without any kind of warning, he stalked to the bed, set her on her feet beside it, and stripped her naked in the space of a heartbeat.

"Mine," he growled. "And when you're in our room, you get naked and stay that way until I give you leave to be otherwise."

The sound he made sent shivers down her spine, but they weren't from fear. No. Gabriella was more turned on than she'd ever been in her life.

Before she could protest, he spun her around and shoved her face first onto the mattress. Didn't Desi say they mounted you from behind before taking the nape of your neck into—what had she called it?—right, a claiming bite.

The hand smacking her right butt cheek hard shouldn't have been a surprise, and yet it was. The sound reverberated off the stone walls. Her mind barely had time to process it before heat and pain bloomed across her ass. Without time for her to even catch her breath, Anders smacked her other cheek and then began a rhythmic set of strikes, each seeming to be harder than the last and covering every single bit of her ass.

If Anders Jensen knew how to kiss, he knew even more about delivering a disciplinary spanking. Each time his hand struck harder than before, delivering pain that blossomed into a deep ache and rippled out from the original strike zone. Over and over, he rained hellfire down on her naked, vulnerable ass until she was crying and asking, not begging, but asking him to stop.

"I know you're upset," she started.

"I was upset when I came to and discovered you gone. I was upset when I couldn't find you. I was upset that you chose to dishonor your family and not come to your sister's wedding. I was upset when I knew you had come back into Norway. What I felt when we rose up over that hill and saw those four men closing in on you was not upset, mate. It was anger, fear and a sense of righteousness about blistering your pretty bottom before I mounted and claimed you as mine."

Anders grabbed her hips and pulled her up on the bed, positioning her so that she was kneeling on the edge as he pushed her head and shoulders into the mattress. He let go of her only long enough to divest himself of his own clothing. He forced her legs apart, stepping between them as the large plum-shaped head of his cock parted her labia and he surged forward, making her cry out in response. Gabriella wasn't sure if it was pleasure and surprise or pain and shock that made her do so.

All she knew was that nothing had ever felt better or more right as Anders Jensen shoved into her, seating his cock deep so that his hard body was tight up against her well-spanked backside.

The visual from her window that night had not done him justice, nor had it prepared her for the feeling of fullness that came from his enormous cock. As he drew back and pressed forward again, she wondered when he'd had time to roll on a condom. Besides, Anders Jensen didn't strike her as a man given to wearing one, ribbed or not. She wasn't overly worried as Desi had said he hadn't been with anyone in over six months and neither had she and she'd been on the pill for years.

The feeling of nubs rubbing against her inner walls was incredibly erotic and she wondered why she'd never wanted a man to wear one of the fancy ones as opposed to something just thin and slick. The second time he drew back, those wonderfully tickling nubs somehow became longer, stiffer and plowed furrows in her tender flesh. Gabriella cried out as Anders held her steady. She tried getting to at least her elbows and earned another smack to her already painful ass and his hand ran up her spine until he held the nape of her neck in his fist and pressed her down.

As angry and aroused as he had to be, Anders didn't seem to want to hurry this. Each time he pressed in, the nubs were much smaller and just teased and stimulated her delicate flesh, but when he grasped her hips and pulled back, those little nubs became painful barbs. Gabriella recalled with clarity once reading about the reason felines yowl so loudly when their mate takes his pleasure was because of the barbs all along his cock.

Some integral part of Anders was a snow leopard, and right now, she was quite certain which part that was. He was much larger than any man she'd ever taken before, and she had the added issue of not having fucked in quite some time, as well as those damn spikes that lined his cock.

Her body responded in a purely feral manner. She moaned and sighed as he began to take long, hard, slow strokes. She relaxed her body and capitulated to him. He was dominant, she was submissive, at least to him.

Grasping both of her hips in his hands, Anders growled, which spoke to some deep, dark primitive part of her psyche. It didn't matter what had brought them together—didn't even matter that she had thought she didn't want this. Anders had known all along they belonged to each other and as he leaned forward to cover her body with his, growling low and quietly as he surged forward, she felt a swift, powerful orgasm wash over her. In spite of herself, Gabriella yowled as he thrust inside her all the way to the base of his cock.

He paused, allowing her to ride the crest of her climax and to allow her body to adjust itself to his as he pulsed inside her, strong and hard. She may have come, but it felt as if he was a long way off. While a part of her appreciated and was grateful that he was letting her catch her breath, there was another, more primal, instinct that needed to be satiated. She wanted everything Anders Jensen had to give her. She needed to feel him thrusting hard in and out of her, sinking his fangs into her neck and claiming her as his fated mate.

Anders held her steady as he began to pound into her, the barbs rippling along her inner walls as he pressed forward and then straightening and strengthening as he drew back, digging into the tender flesh of her wet heat. Dragging himself back, she yowled again in climactic response as he drove forward, before waiting a beat and withdrawing. This was unlike anything she'd ever experienced, ever even heard of before.

Gabriella felt the moment he ceded control and allowed the beast inside to come to the party. The snow leopard that resided within him didn't care for niceties or civilities. All it knew was it wanted to fuck.

It wanted to take its mate and make her pay for the damage she had caused, wanted to ensure she knew who was alpha and who was not.

With a strong and steady rhythm, he began to plunge in and out of her—hard, rough, possessive. The barbs caused pain and pleasure that intermingled and became one. He fucked in and out, pounding her pussy. As his cock found her sweet spot and hammered, sending her flying a third time, her yowling filled the room.

Once again, Anders leaned over, covering her body with his own as he drove into her ruthlessly and relentlessly, not seeming to care that her orgasms were now crashing into each other as he began drawing forth a sustained and primal response from his mate. She barely had time to breathe as he picked up his already furious pace. He nuzzled her neck.

"Mine," he growled again, and she knew what Desi meant, it was as if the sound had a direct line to her pussy.

He moved her hair, baring her neck, and she stiffened. She knew what was coming and it scared the shit out of her. Not only did she not relish the idea of having him sink his fangs into her, the idea of becoming something not quite human was a bit daunting.

As if he could read her mind, the growl became a purr, which was even more devastating as everything in her responded to this man. He surged into her with a last brutal thrust and simultaneously sank his fangs into the nape of her neck, claiming her as his. She felt as though something snapped into life and it was as if she had joined with him and truly become one.

Anders loosened his hold only to bite down more deeply, holding himself tight against her as he pumped his seed deep inside. The warmth of his cum filled her and soothed the ravaged walls of her pussy. It was as if she had always been empty and only he could make her whole. Her pussy contracted all around his cock as it greedily ensured he had nothing left to give her.

Finally, he released his hold on her neck, purring loudly as he nuzzled, licked, and kissed the bite mark, remaining inside her long after he'd finished. Anders withdrew from her, lifting her up and laying her down on the mattress—his eyes raking her body with renewed lust. He placed a finger on her lips to silence her.

"Were I you, my mate, I would try not to arouse my anger again," he crooned.

"What then, would you have me do?" she all but purred at him.

He leaned down, kissing her in a soft, seductive wave that seemed to rev her libido back to life. "Much better," he whispered. "Close your eyes and rest while I order us something to eat. I have claimed you and you are mine, mistress to our clan and I will teach you the ways of our kind." He kissed her again. "I am glad you are home, mate. Should you ever run again, I will lay a set of welts across your ass before I fuck it."

Gabriella knew she should be outraged, knew she should call him every dirty name she could think of, knew she should fight him tooth and nail, but she didn't have it in her. As Desi had suggested, it was long past time she admitted the truth to herself.

"You might have done better just then to tell me you loved me."

"But I did, and I do."

"Nope, not good enough. I want those three little words," she teased, surprised the euphoria left over from the multiple orgasms showed no sign of waning.

"You do not tell me what to do, Gabriella. I am alpha here and you are my mate."

She pointed to the door. "Maybe out there and maybe sexually at all times, but if you were expecting quiet and submissive, boy, did you just claim the wrong girl."

He chuckled, kissing her again. "No, I chose the right girl; and yes, my beautiful mate, my magnificent Rella, I love you."

"Well, then," she purred. "That's all right. How about you order whatever food it is you want to eat, and we go for round two while we're waiting."

"Pace yourself, my mate. We are in seclusion, and I mean to avail myself of your beauty and lush body until I have to carry you down the stairs when we rejoin the clan."

He called down to ask that food be sent up at regular intervals, placed on the floor in the hallway and letting them know it was there by softly knocking on the door.

"Anders?"

"Yes, my beloved?"

"Thanks for saving my life up there."

"I could do nothing less. You and I are now bound together through this life and all the lives to come."

He stood at the edge of the bed, looking down at her, his cock already beginning to recover. Grabbing her ankles, he swirled her around on the bed as he sank to the floor in front of her.

"It would seem my appetite won't wait. I shall have to feast upon you."

He lowered his mouth to her sex and began to do just that and Gabriella forgot why it was she had ever wanted to be anywhere but here with this man.

CHAPTER 18

Sunlight filtered through the windows, warming her skin, but not as much as the length of warm flesh behind her. Gabriella inhaled slowly and held her breath. No, there was definitely someone sleeping next to her. She could hear his breathing... well that, and feel the arm wrapped around her middle. And there was that hard cock that kept nudging her. Although it thinking it needed more was ridiculous. Not that she hadn't enjoyed every single bit of the night before.

The last thing she remembered was cuddling up next to Anders, his body spooned against hers as she lay close to him, replete from the number of times he had made love to her. No, don't think of it in those romantic terms—the number of times he'd pulled her to him and fucked her, or eaten her, or fed her his cock. Each time had left her writhing and crying out his name as she came over and over and over again.

It had been, in some ways, humiliating to have him be able to undo her so easily and completely. And in others it had been the most erotic, sensual, and intimate night of her life. Gabriella could have dismissed the physical experience completely if that was all it had been, but it hadn't. Anders had engaged her heart, her mind, and her very soul—conquering them with ease and leaving nothing for her but the bleak realization that she had surrendered to him.

She wanted to wallow, if not in self-loathing then at least in self-condemnation. This was not what she had envisioned for her life—to be the sexual plaything for a man like Anders Jensen. At least that's what she tried to tell herself. She dismissed out of hand the times he had either tried or succeeded in telling her he loved her. She didn't want to believe it; couldn't allow herself to.

Oh my God! Did I actually let Anders Jensen, leader of the Valhalla Syndicate bite me? Holy shit! What was I thinking?

She could feel, more than hear, the soothing purr resonating down the—what had Anders called it? The tether or bonding link. Shit! Didn't he say he could feel what she was feeling as well? Did that mean he could read her mind? Did he have to be awake to do that? What the hell had she done?

Maybe that wasn't a purr. Maybe that was just the normal light snoring many men, or women for that matter, made when they were sleeping deeply. Gabriella opened one eye. Nope. She hadn't dreamed a castle; it was right there—stone walls, deep set windows and the like. Maybe she was still dreaming. She had dreamed of the enigmatic mafia don every night for the last six months. Did they still call themselves that? Had they ever? Maybe that was just one more fiction invented by novelists and screenwriters.

Gabriella's thoughts were jumbled together. They raced through her mind, rushing down different tracks and colliding into each other. One message that was loud and clear amid her chaotic musings: she needed to get out of Sabu Stronghold, out of Norway, maybe even out of Europe all together.

Leaving Europe sounded like the safest option. Gabriella began to think of all the things she'd need to do. The most difficult would be to tell Zofia, of whom she'd grown fond, that she would not be able to track down her family's stolen painting. The enormity of that crashed down on Gabriella with the weight of a burial stone. Not only did she not want to disappoint Zofia, but there were also all the other families to consider.

Gabriella had two angels sitting on her shoulders. On the left was the one who reminded her of the incredible way Anders had made her feel the night before—not just in giving her the multiple orgasms—but loved and cherished. That angel also reminded her that if she stayed, she could help

Zofia and the survivors and their descendants. Perhaps Anders would be willing to fund hunts for other lost treasures. And there was Desi. Her sister was here and thriving—would it be so bad to be together?

On the other shoulder sat the angel who reminded her she was no longer human and that she could blame Anders for that. No, that wasn't fair or strictly true. She hadn't consented to be turned into a creature that could shift between human and beast. But then again, she hadn't exactly tried to fight him off. That angel reminded her of the barbs that covered his cock unless he suppressed them, which felt amazing as he thrust in, but not so much when he withdrew. Although, as he'd said, she'd gotten used to it and after a while, if she was being honest, had begun to find pleasure in the sensation.

The angel on that shoulder was not amused with the way she countered each of its arguments. 'Fine' it said, he was still a gangster. And to that she had nothing to say.

The arm that had been draped over her midsection tightened and pulled her close as his hand slid down to cup her mons.

"You're discontent, Gabriella. Tell me what's wrong," He rumbled in her ear as he nuzzled her neck.

"Nothing," she said, trying to pull away.

"Do not lie to me. I can not only feel the stiffness

in your body, but I can feel the turmoil in your thoughts and feelings as they flood the tether."

She struggled to turn around so that she was facing him. "All right, if you must know I'm not comfortable with our relationship."

"Had you not managed to elude me for the last six months, you would already have reconciled yourself."

She brought her hands up between them and pushed away from him. She didn't get far, but she was fairly sure he got the message as he growled at her.

"Does it bother you at all that you didn't ask me if I wanted any of this?" she said, exasperated and trying to keep the concern from her voice.

"No, because you would have said no, and that is not an answer I was willing to accept."

Gabriella tried to move away from him, to get some kind of distance between them physically as well as emotionally, but at best it was ineffectual.

"You can't just decide that you're going to keep me prisoner. Someone is bound to start looking for me."

"Not necessarily. People, most especially women and children, go missing all the time and are never heard from again. Usually with children there is some kind of notice—either an Amber Alert or something similar, but you would be surprised at the number of women that simply vanish. Some are murdered, some are sold into slavery, some choose to disappear. My point is that little is done after the initial rush of those left behind reporting it."

"You sound like you know an awful lot about it."

"I do. I make it my business to know. Are you suggesting I am involved in human trafficking or that I condone it? I can assure you, nothing could be further from the truth. Your sister is hoping that perhaps the two of you can do something that would help these women and children—from finding them to helping them establish new lives. Neither Nils nor I will allow you to be actively involved with going up against those who buy and sell them, but if this is something you'd like to do, we can find a way for you to do so safely."

"Will allow? Where do you get off thinking you can tell me what to do or say?"

"I am your mate and your alpha. You will find that my word is law, and you will obey," he said, his voice growing agitated and angry. Gabriella shoved against his chest and was rewarded with a smack to her ass. "Enough, Rella. Settle down." Closing his eyes, he inhaled slowly and pulled her closer. "I feel your fear. We will figure it out."

She shook her head. "No. I don't want to be like you," she said, her voice beginning to crack with the depth of her fear.

Anders smoothed her hair back, pushing it away from her face. His eyes were a curious combination of both steely determination and sympathy. "Calm yourself, Rella. Everything will be fine. I know it's a lot…"

"A lot? You stole my humanity from me."

"I did nothing of the sort. I simply added to that humanity. I have done nothing bad to you. Should you choose to never shift, that is entirely up to you. The snow leopard part of your soul can be repressed. You will live longer and healthier. Should you choose to embrace this new facet of who you are, you will find your senses sharpened and be able to help keep yourself safe."

"Let go of me!"

"Ask me nicely, and I will allow you to leave our bed while I get our food from the hallway. I think I heard a knock a few minutes ago."

"Let go," she growled.

"Ask nicely," he responded calmly.

She took a deep breath, exhaling slowly. "Fine. Anders, will you please allow me to get up?"

Leaning into her, he brushed his lips across her lips, her eyes, and her forehead. "Yes, my beautiful mate, you may leave our bed for a bit."

The instant he released his hold of her, Gabriella all but jumped out of the bed, backing across the room until she was flat against the far wall.

"Gabriella," he said consolingly. "Nothing has changed."

"Nothing? Nothing? You made me some kind of hybrid creature—neither wholly human nor completely snow leopard. You've told me you will never let me go and that I am to be your mate? I had a life, Anders. A damn good one and I am supposed to give up all that and just service you sexually whenever you want?"

He moved to her side of the bed and rolled up into a sitting position, regarding her with a crooked head. "When did I ever say that?"

"Say what?"

"That I expect you to do nothing other than be my personal sex slave. Granted I find nothing wrong with that idea and if that's what you want, I have no objection, but I knew who you were when I took you in a claiming bite."

He stood up, not bothering to pull on any clothes. Why should he? She was naked as well. And while she could attribute her pebbled nipples to the chill in the air, his stiffening cock was caused by only one thing. The real problem was that she knew her nipples weren't in their current state because she was cold and even if they were, she damn sure couldn't blame the way her pussy was getting soft and wet on the temperature.

Anders opened the door and bent down to retrieve the tray of food. Damn, he had a fine ass. It was muscular and, as she recalled, felt good in her hands when she'd used it to pull him closer. The memory of doing so flashed through her mind and she could feel a blush creeping up her cheeks. He stood and turned, his cock now almost fully erect. She couldn't decide which looked more appetizing—the food, which smelled delicious, or his hard cock, which she knew felt like nothing she'd experienced before.

"I'm not sure how to interpret that look," he said, smiling at her.

Of course, he was smiling. Everything was going his way and he'd always been a snow leopard, or had he?

"Anders, are you born a snow leopard or did someone have to bite you?"

He chuckled as he put the tray down on the table beside the armchair and beckoned to her. "Come sit with me."

"I'm fine where I am."

"Learn to choose your battles with me, Rella. We both know I can make you sit in my lap and if I have to do that, you will straddle me with my cock up your cunt while we eat." He waited a moment and then continued. "Now."

There was no mistaking the note of command in his voice. She knew he was right and knew that he wasn't making an idle threat, but the very idea of sitting in his lap, impaled on his cock, had a certain appeal. Another long sigh and she ambled over to him.

God what had happened to her?

CHAPTER 19

Anders reminded himself that this was all new to her. She was right that she hadn't given him her consent. He hadn't even asked her. He had known they were fated mates and he was tired of waiting for her. He wanted her bound to him in as many ways as he could think of. He heard the long sigh, saw the slight slump to her shoulders and could feel her tumultuous thoughts churning inside her head through the bonding link.

He knew it was too soon to use the tether overtly to try and soothe her; still, he emitted a low rumbling purr that she could hear and feel as well.

"Why do you do that?" she asked bleakly as she stood before him.

"Because whatever you may think of me now, I want you to be happy. I don't want you to be upset."

"Then you shouldn't have turned me," she said quietly, but with absolute surety.

"You are wrong, Rella. You gave me no choice but to turn you without waiting for your consent, which you would have given me in the end."

"No choice? Really? Did I miss the guy with a gun to your head?" she asked, her tone becoming more agitated and upset.

"You ran away and then managed to elude me for months. When I finally located you, four men had ambushed you and would have killed you had we not come for you. So, if anyone has had a gun to my head in the last six months, it is you. Now sit down in my lap, let's have breakfast and I will answer any questions you have."

"I'm not a child to be pulled into your lap, fed some amazing food, and told a fairytale."

Anders laughed. "I have no interest in treating you like a child. I want you in my lap because it pleases me to have you there. I know I took you far more times than I should have last night, but it has been a long time since I took a woman to my bed. You have to be hungry."

"What's long? A week? Ten days?" she said spitefully.

"That is the first, last, and only time you accuse me of infidelity. Since the moment I knew you were my fated mate, I have not so much as touched another woman. And I figured that out long before we met in Paris."

He could see he'd surprised her. Her eyes widened and her pupils dilated. Good. If he could challenge her assumptions about that, he could challenge them about other things.

Gabriella sat down in his lap and wriggled around until she was comfortable. He wondered fleetingly if she had done that deliberately to torture him, His cock was desperately reminding him that before last night, the only relief it had been given was via his hand. When she reached for a piece of bacon, he slapped her hand, lightly.

"No, Rella, when you sit in my lap, I will feed you." He took the piece of bacon she had tried to pick up and brought it to her lips. Shaking her head, she took a bite. She was annoyed with him, but not afraid, and even her anger had lost its edge. "What is it you would like to know?"

"Don't lie to me, Anders. If you do, I will never trust you."

"Do you trust me now?" he asked, needing to hear her answer.

"I trust you to be who I know you to be, but I need to know that at least for this morning, when I ask you questions, I will get a truthful answer."

He nodded. It was honest—not everything he hoped for, but honest. "Begin."

"Is it painful to be turned into someone like you?"

His first instinct was to give her a witty response, but he could feel it was bothering her that she didn't know what to expect. Had he waited for her consent, he most likely would have already covered this ground. At least in this, she deserved the truth.

"The most painful part has already happened. The bite is the worst of it. You may feel a general malaise, but if it happened to you without any knowledge, you probably would attribute it to an over-indulgence the night before."

He scooped up a bit of the excellent seafood hash and offered it to her. She took a bite and seemed to enjoy it.

"Okay. How did you become a… shit, I don't even know what to call it."

"We either refer to ourselves as shifters or snow leopards. As for how I became one, I was born that way, as were most who live here."

"That takes care of my next question. So, does that bite mean I'm your concubine?"

He chuckled as he continued to feed her. "What a charming notion, but no. Like your sister did with Nils, we will be legally wed."

"Do I get any say-so about that?"

"About whether or not we're getting married? Not really. If you're really opposed to the convention of marriage, we can just have a bonding ceremony although they are very similar, but you will take your vows to me in front of witnesses."

"When?"

"I suppose if you want a really large wedding, I could manage to wait six months. But the more direct answer is the sooner, the better."

"Which brings us back to my original question—how did you become a snow leopard?"

"I was born as one. My family have been snow leopards for thousands of years. Our clan isn't as large as others, but our bloodline is purer. In general, we stick to our own kind unless one of us is called to a fated mate who is human."

"How do you recognize a 'fated mate'? I don't recall seeing anything that labeled me as such."

He grinned. "Baiting me is not going to work often and when it does, you'll usually feel my discipline. But males know from the first moment they draw breath whether or not the Goddess…"

"Goddess? Are you pagans?"

Anders shrugged. "Some are; some aren't. The legends say that during the time of the Gods, Freyja chose her familiars to carry on and protect her people. Each became a shifter—the ice lion, the snow leopard, and the winter tiger."

"Did you just divide up Norway?"

"No. The ice lion is Gunnar Madsen of the Blood Eagle Syndicate, and he is the guardian of Denmark. I'm the snow leopard, and am the sentinel not only of Sabu, but the entire country. Sweden is the home of Lars Jakobssen, the winter tiger, of the Berserker

Syndicate."

"You're awfully quick to give up your compatriots."

"I have no concerns. If you were going to tell anyone about our existence, you would have done so by now. Other regions have other goddesses who did the same. I find it fascinating that it is always a goddess who seeks to protect those she will leave behind."

"You said males are born knowing. What about females? Is it tattooed on the guy's dick?"

Tossing back his head he laughed. "That sounds painful, and no. That wouldn't work."

"Why not—not the tattooing but the females knowing."

"Because females don't have the ability to turn a human into a shifter."

"That sounds rather unfair," she said with a bit of a sneer.

"I suppose it does. But I don't know of any shifters who aren't patriarchal in nature. Men rule; women follow."

"Well, isn't that just ducky… if you're a man."

"I won't disagree, and I have known more than one shifter clan that would be better off with one of their females in charge. There are those who say women are too emotional to lead. I don't agree with that. A she-cat or she-wolf or whatever can be as ruthless as any of her male counterparts. In fact,

Gunnar recently named his fated mate his beta, and the rumor is when the bratva attacked Hammerfall, she led a group of those who defended the castle and won the day. For what it's worth, I think you'll like Marley. She is the younger sister of Joshua, the Lion of London."

"What about this Lars fellow?"

"The winter tiger? I've always thought Berserker Syndicate was fitting. Lars can be great fun to be around, but if you cross him, he can be brutal."

"As opposed to your kind and benevolent way of doing things?" she said with sweet sarcasm.

"Precisely," he said, ignoring her jab.

"Why is it necessary to turn your mate?" she asked thoughtfully.

"Because unless you are truly one with me, you cannot bear my children."

"Do you want children?"

"Yes, but that is a discussion we will need to have."

"Does one of your sons automatically become leader?"

He shook his head. "Not necessarily. Generally speaking, the mantle of alpha is passed father to son, but anyone can challenge the reigning alpha. The winner either becomes alpha or remains as such."

"What happens to the loser?"

"If both are adult males, the fight is generally to the death. If one is a child, he and his mother and any siblings are banished."

"So, you assumed the job upon your father's death?"

"No. As I told you I studied at the Cordon Bleu. I had just graduated when my father was killed by my uncle, his younger brother. My mother was dead, and I had no siblings. Nils left his family and joined me in exile. I watched and waited for a number of years until I felt strong enough—both physically and with enough support within the clan. Then I challenged my uncle."

"You killed your own uncle?" she said with a shiver.

"I want there to be no secrets between us. So, yes, but he gave me no choice. I had defeated him and had the support of the clan. He tried to stab me in the back. My snow leopard must have heard him coming and flashed forward to protect me. I instinctively ripped his throat out. He had no mate or children. I have led the clan since I was in my early twenties. It is not a responsibility I take lightly."

He could sense the shift in her from appalled and fearful, to loving and compassionate as she put her arms around him, and he could feel the vaguest rumblings of a purr coming from her down the tether to soothe him.

"That must have been awful for you. This bonding link thing. I think I could feel what you felt then. You took no pleasure or pride in killing him and you did what you did to protect your clan, not in revenge for your father. That's a terrible burden to place on a young man."

Anders hugged her close, glad of her nearness. "You are the only one who has ever understood that. Thus the reason I need you with me. The alpha's mate is the only one who ever truly understands the burden that he carries."

"And perhaps by sharing that burden, she takes a little of the weight off him."

He nodded. "You are my fated mate, Gabriella. I cannot lead this clan and protect our people—not just those here at Sabu or in the town below, but in all of Norway—without you. I must know you are safe."

Gabriella kept her arms around him and purred as she nuzzled his neck, and then picked up the fork he had placed on the tray beside the plate and used it to offer him some more of the seafood hash. Anders knew it wasn't much, but he couldn't help but feel it was a start in the right direction.

CHAPTER 20

She couldn't even imagine having gone through what he had. To know his uncle had deliberately slain his father. Gabriella wasn't overly fond of her father's brother, but she knew he would never stoop to kill him. She smiled as she leaned into Anders' strength.

"Why the smile?" he asked.

"I was just thinking how awful it must have been for you, and simultaneously understanding why you and Nils are so close…"

"He is like a brother to me."

"My father's side of the family isn't overly fond of my mother. She, on the other hand, positively loathes them."

He chuckled. "Your mother is a formidable woman. The good news is, she rather likes me."

"According to Desi, she adores you and was disappointed Desi had—her words, not mine—settled for Nils."

"Understandable. She would want her daughter to make the best match, which in her eyes would be the one who has the castle. She'll be happy to know you've finally decided to settle down and marry. Both she and your father worry about you. Don't get me wrong, they are proud of the work you do, but your mother doesn't understand it. Your father does, though."

Gabriella nodded. "I know. But then it was my paternal great-grandmother's diaries of her exploits during the war and afterward that started me down this road. I have to help Zofia."

"And I suppose you expect me to fund this little adventure of yours, minus keeping the painting."

"You don't know what retrieving these pieces of art stolen by Nazis means to these people. For some it is the only tangible link to what their families endured and/or lost. Sometimes they are willing to sell if the price is right…"

"Then I'll make them an offer they can't refuse."

Gabriella looked down at him askance. Seeing his laughing eyes, she batted at him. "That's not funny."

"In that case, my beauty," he said, standing and lifting her in his arms, "I shall have to make do with claiming my consolation prize—a snow leopard from Sabu."

Anders walked back to the bed and laid her down.

Covering her body with his own, he proceeded to do just that.

~

The next few days flew by in an erotic blaze that wrapped itself around them as Gabriella began to trust the growing bond between them and let go of the anger she had tried so hard to hold on to in order to shield her heart from his sensual onslaught. Anders was a strong, virile, and tactile lover and preferred to have her close at all times.

At first, she found the bonding link invasive, but little by little, as he used it to reveal the most secret parts of himself to her, she began to enjoy the intimacy that it created. She opened her eyes to sunlight streaming through the French doors that led out onto their private balcony.

Sometime during the night, they had shifted positions and instead of Anders being spooned against her, he was lying on his back with his arm around her, holding her close. Gabriella had her head on his shoulder with her arm across his torso. She felt the heat of his flesh against her skin, warming her even with the bedclothes tossed back in the chilly room. The man was a virtual furnace, and she knew she'd never be cold again.

She heard his purr before he spoke. "Did you sleep well?"

"What little you let me get," she teased.

"Such is the life of being mate to the alpha. We're demanding bastards."

"According to my sister, it isn't just the alphas."

"Is she complaining?" he asked languidly.

Gabriella suspected he already knew the answer. "No, and for the record, I wasn't complaining, either."

He chuckled softly, giving her a squeeze. "Good; because in that area, I'm afraid it will do you no good."

One thing about Anders: he always made her feel as if she were the only woman in the world he wanted. When she was with him, even before she had known who he was, he had made her feel safe, sexy, desirable, and that he valued her for her intelligence as much as anything else.

Gabriella stretched up, bringing her mouth to his and letting her tongue run along the seam of his lips until they parted, and then slid it inside his mouth to tangle with his. Anders shivered but refrained from taking control. Making love with this man was like no one else before. He was dominating, sometimes overwhelmingly so, but instead of intimidating her or making her resent it, he was teaching her to glory in her submissiveness—to be empowered by it and embrace the way it made her feel.

Wet. Wet, soft, and ready was how it made her

feel. Her senses sang when she was in Anders' arms, and he provided the perfect harmony.

~

Anders knew they were on borrowed time. They'd been in seclusion for three days and three nights. He hadn't allowed her to get dressed, hadn't allowed her to not be within reach. His decision to tell her about his uncle with the link wide open had been the right one. Gabriella could be physically aroused, but in order to seduce his mate, he had to show her that he, too, was vulnerable.

He nudged her onto her back, rolling on top of her as he did so. He spread her legs with his own, making a place for himself amidst her softness. She had the most amazing hazel eyes. At times they were more golden brown; at others, an almost catlike shade of green. He had known she was his fated mate. He'd been unprepared for all that entailed.

He didn't just want to fuck her; didn't just want to sire his children with her. No, he was a greedy bastard and he wanted it all. He wanted her to love him and if that meant changing some things and some of the ways he did business, then so be it. Sometimes all a man needed was the right mate to teach him what was right and true. And if he was smart, he would never let her get away.

He lowered his lips to hers, demanding they part

and allow his tongue to plunge past her teeth to taste and explore and enjoy. There was a heady feeling of euphoria that overcame her when he made love to her, and he knew it to be just that. Lovemaking. It wasn't that she shied away from the raw, primitive feral side of him, it was just that even then, he could feel the love underscoring her lust. Making it more.

He knew he loved her, but sensed she wasn't ready to hear that, even though he had told her once before. He would wait a while longer before he forced the issue. He would bind her to him with their vows and with sex. He would make her crave him the way he craved her. She felt so damn good as he sank into her. Gabriella cried out, arching her body and raking his back with her nails, orgasming just from his possession. If he was a wild beast, she was his feral alley cat in heat.

She was unlike anyone he'd known before. Oh, sure, he'd had pulse-pounding sex with a lot of women, but they were nothing compared to her. Gabriella was a force of nature—strong, proud, intelligent and the most beautiful thing he'd ever seen. He was aware that her older sister was the type of woman other women aspired to be, but she was too thin to his way of thinking. Gabriella was soft and round with luscious curves and a body meant to give a man pleasure.

He knew she didn't relish the idea of being kept safe, but he didn't care. Those men had meant to kill her—two Russians; two Germans. He didn't like the way that sounded. And why were they after her? It had to be she was closing in on the cache of stolen Nazi art. None of that mattered; he knew what Gabriella needed—him.

Lowering his forehead to hers, he thrust inside her even more deeply. God, she felt glorious. She was every dream, every fantasy, and yet, she was real; more importantly, she was *his*. He began to draw back before thrusting in again. This time when he began to withdraw, he allowed the barbs to come out to rake her inner walls. Nothing had ever felt this good... this right. He would take care of her and protect her whether she liked it or not.

Angling his pelvis down, he began to hit her clit with every other stroke. Gabriella held him close, first scoring his back with her nails and then grabbing his ass, trying to pull him in deeper. Her body had become accustomed to his and she felt perfect as he stroked in and out of her with a surety and ease that should have taken months, if not years, to find, but it had been this way from the first time he drove his cock inside her.

Gabriella writhed beneath him, trying to get him to stay deep and, he knew, find his own orgasm. But this felt too good. There was far too much pleasure to be had in fucking his mate. Regardless of how hard she tried she could not keep him from pounding into her with a relentless rhythm he knew she loved. Her body tightened as she arched her back and dug her nails into his skin.

Her pussy threatened to strangle his cock from the intensity of her orgasm. So much so that he lost control for only a moment and his cock took over, driving deep in a final ferocious thrust before spilling himself into her. Nothing had ever felt as good as flooding her pussy with his cum as her inner walls trembled, milking him to get every last drop.

Peace settled over them. He could feel it thrumming between them along the tether. He allowed himself to rest on her, giving her his full weight as she sighed contentedly. He never wanted to leave this moment, this intimate place. The world outside could fade away and never intrude again. He would remain here… with her.

A loud knock on the door sounded. Well, so much for that.

CHAPTER 21

Another knock and the door cracked open, "Alpha?" called Nils without sticking his head in. Anders made no move to withdraw from her.

"This had better be damned important," he growled, still inside her and showing no intention of getting off.

"Make him go away," she whispered.

"Nils? She wants me to cut off your head."

"Anders! That is not what I said."

"Forgive me, mistress. Were it not an urgent matter, I would not disturb you. Gunnar Madsen and Lars Jakobsson have initiated a video call and wish to speak with you."

Anders looked down at her. "I suppose you'd object to my taking the call as I am, or better yet sitting up with you impaled on my cock." She rolled her eyes and he chuckled as he withdrew, "You wait here, and don't move. I'll be back."

She was still mesmerized by the way he moved. For a large, muscle-bound man, he moved with such predatory grace.

"Nils? Is my sister available?" called Gabriella.

"I told you to wait," Anders growled.

"You go talk to your friends and I will assure my sister that you haven't broken me," she retorted.

"I assure you, Mistress, that thought never crossed her mind," said Nils, the amusement apparent in his tone.

Anders headed into their bath, took a quick shower and emerged, quickly pulling on jeans and a deep V-neck sweater in moss green that complemented his coloring perfectly. He leaned over her, giving her a quick hard kiss as his hand stroked down her body and tugged her clit.

"You and your sister behave."

He walked out of the door and pulled it closed behind him. She got up and headed into the shower. She used the sea sponge and then the scrubby with bath gel and could still smell his scent on her. Gabriella wondered if that was because of her enhanced senses or just the fact that in the past three days there hadn't been a moment when he wasn't touching her in some way. The man was positively obsessed with her, which was good, as she felt the same way about him.

She came out of the bath with one towel wrapped around her and drying her hair with another. She smiled as she spotted Desiree sitting on the edge of her bed, having pulled the covers up.

"It's about time the two of you came up for air. God, it reeks of sex in here," Desiree said instead of saying hello.

"Love you, too. I rather imagine your bedroom is the same."

"I know—isn't it great? You are happy, aren't you?"

"I don't know that I'm happy yet, but I'm not resentful and I don't know that I have a choice."

"He loves you," stated Desiree. "He was positively miserable without you."

"So he tells me," Gabriella said. "I think we'll be fine. I do have feelings for him—strong, good ones."

"Everyone has been pumping me for information. They know he claimed you. There are several of us who shift every morning and go for a run. Want to come along?"

"I've never done that. Never even tried."

"It's really easy. I can teach you."

Deciding in for a penny, in for a pound, she nodded. "What the hell? Let's give it a go."

"Excellent. You should know you can shift with your clothes on, but when you shift back, you'll be naked. Normally what we all do is meet in the changing room downstairs at the back of the keep and then shift and run together, but you can shift up here if you prefer."

"Why don't we do that but grab something for me to change into when we come back."

"Okay. So, to shift, just find a quiet place in your mind. You'll be able to feel her kind of lurking in the background. When you see her, just call to her; think of shifting; she'll charge towards you and leap. All you need to do is let go and when you open your eyes, you'll be a snow leopard."

"That sounds easy enough."

"It is," Desi assured her. "The trick is not to flinch or try to push her away when she makes the leap."

"Okay. Here we go," said Gabriella, closing her eyes and trying to find that quiet place she'd always had when she did yoga or tried to meditate.

Desiree was right. As soon as she slowed her breathing and synchronized it with her heartbeat, she could feel the presence of another entity. It was as if she was prowling just along the fringes of her mind. Gabriella allowed herself to be open to her presence and called to her. As Desiree had said, the beautiful snow leopard walked into view, looking at her as if to determine whether or not she was worthy. Deciding she was, the beautiful creature began to trot toward her, picking up speed until she was galloping, and then she leaped.

It took everything within her not to reject or push the beast away. Instead, she focused on welcoming her and allowing her to take over. Desi had been right about the feeling as well. It was as if Anders had a violet wand in his hand on the lowest setting and was running it all over her body, lighting up her skin and the underlying nerves with a tingling feeling that was intensely pleasurable, bordering on painful.

When she opened her eyes, she could feel that her body was no longer her own. She was on all fours and as she looked down, she could see fur.

"The two hardest things are to remember to retract your claws if you've used them to grab onto something and that you have a long tail. I don't want to tell you how many things I knocked over until I learned to control it. Then you can find all sorts of ways to have fun with it. Try moving around."

That was easier said than done. At first Gabriella felt awkward and clumsy, but as her sister encouraged her and gave her advice, it got easier. Once she was relatively certain she wouldn't make a complete fool of herself, she went to the door and waited for Desi to open it. She followed her sister down the main staircase to the back of the keep. People acknowledged both her and Desi. They called her either Gabriella or Mistress, which she was assuming was her title as mate to the alpha.

They entered the changing room and what had been the sound of feminine voices and laughter became eerily silent.

"I told you, she's not like that," said Desi. "Among

many shifters, the mate to the alpha rules the other females with an iron hand. She hadn't shifted before so kind of wanted to try it out first. See? I have clothes right here; she'll shift back with the rest of us."

Smiling faces began to talk again and bid her welcome to the clan. One by one the women disrobed and shifted into their snow leopard selves. Each came to her and rubbed their cheeks against hers. Gabriella had never felt so accepted.

Desi was the last to shift. "Normally, you'll lead the run, but you don't know the estate yet and the best paths. Sometimes we just take a gentle run, which I thought would be good for today and sometimes we take on the more difficult terrain. If it's okay, I thought you and I could run in the lead together."

Not being able to talk was going to take some getting used to as when she tried all that came out were garbled noises.

"I'm going to take that for a yes."

Gabriella nodded and watched as a silvery cloud with sparks of ice and color consumed her sister before dissipating to reveal her snow leopard. Desi was gorgeous—of course she was. Her fur was snowy white with black speckles and spots throughout. They padded out of the gate together and took off at a run with a pack of ten female snow leopards behind them.

Both Desiree and Anders had tried to describe what it felt like to be in this shifted form and experience the world in a new and different way. She could feel the blades of grass beneath her feet, each one distinct and different yet forming a whole. She thought that was something of a metaphor for being in the clan—each different, with a different skill and experience, but coming together to form an entirely different kind of community.

They ran up into the fields and Gabriella understood why the walls were so high around the estate. Anders wasn't trying to keep any of them in; he was keeping the world out, keeping them safe from prying eyes. They ran through the thick forest and out into the lush pastures. The horses looked up from their grazing, but recognizing these were not predators, went back to nibbling grass.

Leaping over the tall fences was something of a learning experience. Gabriella sort of fell over the first one, got hung up on the second, and missed the third one completely. She heard the other she-cats make a chuffing noise which she understood to be laughter and had to join in with them. The fourth one was a bit better and by the fifth one she had it down pat. When she cleared it easily, her companions rushed to encircle and rub up against her to congratulate her.

She had never been a runner before. It had always felt boring to her but running as a snow leopard was a completely different experience. It was a celebration of life, and she was elated to participate. They ran down one of the easier paths that led to the beach and played in the sand together. Desi was right;

learning to flick sand with her tail was fun and she imagined it could be a useful skill every now and again.

The group of females was running in and out of the water, splashing and frolicking like schoolgirls, when a single loud roar cut through their frivolity, and they all looked up to see a lone male snow leopard standing on top of the craggy cliff. He roared again and the others fled to a different, more direct path back up to the keep. Desi hesitated until Gabriella nudged her with her snout and inclined her head after the others. If Anders wanted to have this out, they could bloody well have it out. She turned her back and ran back into the water until it was belly deep and she began to swim.

It didn't take long for her to hear him splashing into the water behind her. She swam toward a large rock that jutted out of the sea and crawled her way to the top, using her claws to help get her there quickly and remembering to retract them as she turned and sat to watch her mate as he made his way to her.

She reached out along the bonding link but didn't feel what she had expected. Anders was far from annoyed. All she could feel was pride and joy as he clambered up onto the rock to sit close beside her, nuzzling her and rubbing his cheek as the others had done. She inclined her head into his, closed her eyes, and sighed. This, too, felt special and right.

They sat for only a few moments before he stood

and nudged her to do the same. He plunged back into the water and waited for her. Together, they swam back to shore, and he showed her how to use the loose, dry sand to help remove water from her coat and then to shake it off. They ran back up the easier path to the keep, where he led her inside, showing her to the women's changing area and then gallantly taking himself into the men's.

Desiree and several of the others were waiting. "He wasn't angry, was he?" she asked.

Gabriella shook her head.

"Good. I realized I didn't tell you how to shift back. It's not hard and I'm sure you'd have figured it out. But all you do is ask her to let go and return control to you. She should give over and you'll feel the shift come over you," explained Desi. "The first couple of times you shift, it can be exhausting, so we'll wait and make sure you're steady enough to walk."

"Or our alpha will carry you back to his bed," said one of the others with a giggle.

Gabriella closed her eyes and thanked her snow leopard for bonding with her and allowing her to shift and run with her. The snow leopard rubbed up against her in her mind's eye and then receded until once again she was comfortably curled up in the corner by a fire. Smiling, Gabriella opened her eyes and saw that the silver shimmer was already starting to dissipate. She reached out her hand and thought she could feel, for a split second, starlight and eternity.

CHAPTER 22

"That was amazing. Almost as good as sex with Anders," she exclaimed. "Sex with the alpha is definitely better, but damn, that was great." The other women laughed as she pulled on her clothing. "Are you always hungry and horny afterwards?"

"Yes, and luckily the men are pretty much always hungry, horny, and hard," laughed one of the women.

"Too bad," interjected Desi. "Breakfast is being served and you two will be expected to join us."

"Okay. Any idea what that call from Lars and Gomer was about?"

"Gunnar," supplied Desi. "No, but they were fairly insistent."

"I knew it wasn't Gomer."

As they walked into the hall, Anders and several

of the men, including Nils, were there to escort them to breakfast.

"What's wrong?" she whispered.

"Nothing that won't wait until after breakfast," he responded quietly before speaking so the rest could hear him. "You were magnificent as a snow leopard. Even more beautiful than I had imagined."

"Obviously, he didn't see my first few attempts at leaping fences. My personal favorite was when I hooked into the rail by mistake and face planted on the other side," quipped Gabriella.

"But even then, she was beautiful and graceful," said one of the she-cats who had run with her. Gabriella stopped, turned and looked at her, arching an eyebrow. "Well, it was funny, but you were still beautiful."

Anders laughed as he led them into the dining hall. The others dropped back so they entered alone, and Anders presented her to their clan. "May I have the pleasure of introducing you to my fated mate and your mistress, Gabriella, whose sister is our Desiree."

People got to their feet and cheered, calling out greetings and congratulations. Anders led her to the high table, beaming. He pulled out her chair and helped her scoot back in, leaning down to kiss her shoulder.

"You aren't mad I ran without you?" she whispered, suddenly worried he might be and not wanting Desi to get in trouble.

"Not at all, sweetheart. You are safe within the walls of the estate. If that changes, I will let you know. You were truly magnificent. It looked as though you had been born a snow leopard."

They ate breakfast, talking about how much she had enjoyed the run and answering people's questions. It was as if they were home again at a Cajun celebration—loud, long, and full of laughter. After breakfast, Anders asked Desi, Nils, and Gabriella to join him in his study. He led Gabriella with him behind the desk, pulling her into his lap as he sat down in the leather chair behind it.

"As you know, I spoke with Gunnar and Lars this morning. They heard from the Laochra, which is the coalition between England, Ireland, Scotland, and Wales. It seems things have gone from bad to worse. The Odessa…"

"I thought that was just something Frederick Forsyth made up for his novel," said Gabriella.

"I'm afraid not. They existed during WWII and continue to exist today, helping those still alive, their descendants, and those who would carry on," explained Anders. "The Odessa was a covert group of SS officers who helped facilitate the ratlines and with setting up new lives in South America and the Middle East. They have joined forces with the bratva to get to that hidden treasure before anyone else. We don't think they know the exact location, but they think Gabriella is on the right track."

"Thus, the reason some of my would-be assailants…"

"There was nothing 'would be' about them. They didn't succeed, but you were the intended target. They meant to get any information you had and then kill you," snarled Anders.

Gabriella found herself purring softly to him to soothe his anger and agitation. Had the bonding link not been in place, she might have thought he was angry with her. He wasn't, and she knew it.

"Were they behind the shot that was fired in Paris?" she asked.

"We believe so. As I said, the police are pretty sure he was bratva, but he killed himself before they could question him."

"Okay, so twice they tried and twice they failed. And now I'm a snow leopard."

"That will give you speed and strength, but it won't stop a bullet."

"I see your point. But I have to tell you, I don't have anything definitive, just a hunch that it's in Skjult Fjord. It's not like I have a map with a big ole X, marking the spot."

"What do you have?" asked Nils. "Anders and I grew up here, running and riding in all of these fjords. After his father was killed, we couldn't come back, but Anders would not leave the clan or his territory without his protection, so we lived off the land up in the fjords and helped when and where we could."

"It wasn't as noble as he makes it sound," retorted Anders.

"I don't think anyone believes that, babe. Gangster or not, you've got this noble streak about a mile wide. You were alpha in absentia. But you were always alpha," said Gabriella.

Nils smiled at her and then looked at Anders. "Careful, Alpha, your mate already sees into your soul."

Anders nodded. "That she does."

"What I have is a bunch of diagrams and drawings from my great-grandmother's things. The most promising was a map of Skjult Fjord showing three Nazi symbols, which all came from Nordic runes: The Wolfsangel, used to ward off anyone the Nazis thought could defeat them; the Othala rune, and the Algis or Life rune, which they used to symbolize their supposed Aryan purity and bloodline."

"Wouldn't a swastika have been more easily recognized?" asked Desi.

Gabriella nodded. "Yes, too easily. I'm guessing in their arrogance they believed that people would assume they were left there by ancient Norwegians."

"Do you think they're in a hole in the ground?" asked Nils.

"It would have to be in something bigger, like a cavern," answered Gabriella.

"Like a mine shaft?" speculated Anders.

"Yes, that would work well. Why?" asked

Gabriella, the hairs beginning to stand up on the back of her neck.

"Because Nils and I stayed in Skjult Fjord because it is said to be haunted by evil spirits—those Viking warriors who had dishonored themselves and were not allowed into Valhalla. It's a place that people avoid, even if they're able to find it. We found an old mine shaft that had been sealed. I don't remember any symbols, but then we weren't looking for any and would probably have dismissed them, just as the Nazis wanted."

"Can we go there? Today?" asked Gabriella.

Anders nodded. "Nils, let's take the large chopper and say four of our best men. I want everyone armed…"

"You should make sure Gabi and I have guns. We're both really good shots," interjected Desi.

"If so, Desiree is right," said Nils. "Gabriella should have a gun. But you, Desiree, will stay here."

"No way," she argued. "If Gabi gets to go, so do I."

"No, little one. This is dangerous enough as it is, but Gabriella has to go. You do not," growled Nils.

"You do know if you leave her behind, she'll only find a way to follow us, right?" said Gabriella.

"She's right. I will. If I cry prettily and spin them the right story, the men will believe me. A group of them will come, leaving fewer people here to guard the clan. Much better to take me along," Desi added.

"Anders?" asked Nils looking for support.

Anders quirked his eyebrows up. "I suspect my mate knows yours better than you. I'd be inclined to let her come along, but at the first sign of trouble, we get them to the chopper and get them out of there."

"I don't like it," argued Nils.

"Nor do I, but I fear we have little choice. We need to find that cache of treasure."

"Why are the bratva interested in it?" asked Desi.

Anders, Nils, and Gabriella all answered simultaneously. "Money."

"Triple Jinx," called Gabriella and realized Anders and Nils had no idea what she was talking about. "If the bratva can get their hands on part of that, it would be a huge payday for them. I don't think we're going to find all of what's still missing, but I do think we might find at least part of what the Nazis stole from Warsaw." She shook her head to express her uncertainty. "It's got to be worth at least tens, if not hundreds, of millions."

"Nils. Get the men ready and get Gabriella and Desiree vests, as well as guns."

"Anders?"

"I don't like it and it's ultimately your call, but I think it's probably safer to keep them together."

Nils let out a resigned sigh. "Your will; my hand."

Within the hour, Anders had organized his men, ensured that all those that lived within the estate had been brought in and were within the keep, and everyone, including Gabriella and Desiree, had been issued Kevlar vests and automatic weaponry. The six men and two women took horses up to the landing strip and put them in the stable that had been built for housing them there. They climbed into the fully armored, stealth capable helicopter and lifted off.

Gabriella sat up in the seat by the pilot, looking at the map and giving him directions. Eventually, they entered Skjult Fjord and between Gabriella's map and Nils and Anders, they found the entrance to the old mine. They set the chopper down within sight of the mine, but at a safe distance.

Leaving two of the men to keep watch and keep the chopper safe, the two women with the remaining four men walked up to the old mine shaft. Anders and Nils had been right. It was sealed.

They began searching the surrounding field for where they thought the entrance to the mine might be.

"Gabriella," called Anders. "I think I found one of the runes." He began pulling away old foliage and moss from the flat rock.

Gabriella joined him. "Yep. That's Algis. I think we're in the right spot. Fan out. If the Nazis follow their pattern they'll be separated at the boundaries—two at either side on the bottom and then the third at the top so they form a triangle. Let's fan out left and right from this rune."

The search party began to fan out, looking for

rocks of a similar size, which had a flat surface on which the Nazis could have carved their symbols. It was slow going as the size they were searching for wasn't overly large, which made sense if you were trying to keep something hidden as they had been.

Eventually, Berg, one of the men with them, cried out. "I think I found one!"

Berg stepped back and pulled away the overgrowth, tracing the rounded circle with the crossed bottom. She grinned up at Berg. "That's Othala. So, since it is on a straight line from Algis, the Wolfsangel should be at the top... roughly in the middle of this line so that it forms a perfect isosceles triangle."

With renewed vigor they began searching. Gabriella stumbled, tripping over something half buried. Anders caught and steadied her. She began to walk off, but then turned back, kneeling in the dirt where she'd tripped and digging around with her hands. When she found the flat surface of the half-buried rock she slipped her fingers through the vegetation, and let her fingertips find what she was sure would prove to be the Wolfsangel.

Gabriella dug around, removing dirt and foliage until the rock with the symbol was revealed. She turned to Anders. "By Jove, I think we've got it. Now let's start carefully removing dirt and the rest of this stuff. Try not to walk between the two symbols at the bottom."

Desi nodded. "There's no telling what kind of shape the barrier is in."

After close to two hours of back-breaking work, they had dug around the iron doors that led into what they suspected was a long-abandoned mine. Finally, they sat back, each of them taking a drink from a bottle of water. Exhaustion was a steady beat in their veins, but accompanying it was a thrum of awareness, the recognition they had just accomplished something that would alter their world.

CHAPTER 23

Anders took a long draw from his bottle, divided in his thinking. Should he send Gabriella and Desiree back to the relative safety of the chopper, or allow them to see it through?

"No," Gabriella whispered. "You can't ask me to leave you when we're this close."

"I can if I think you are safer with the chopper, and you will obey me," he growled.

Sensing now was not the time to debate equality with her mate, Gabriella said, "Yes, but I've been working on this for a long time. Long before I met Zofia, even. Please, Anders. As long as Desi says it's safe, aren't we better off with you and Nils?"

He shook his head as if he couldn't believe what he was about to say. "We'll need to make sure that it's safe to go inside," said Anders.

"I can help with that, Alpha," said Desiree.

"How so?"

"She's an architect by training; she can give you a good idea whether the thing is structurally sound," answered Gabriella.

"When is it supposed to have been sealed?" asked Desiree, feeling the seams of the door and its casing.

"I'm not sure of the exact date, but back in the sixteenth or seventeenth century."

"No way," said Desi, shaking her head. "The way they sealed it required technology and materials of the twentieth century. No way this was done before, I'd say, 1930 at the earliest, and my closer estimation is the mid-1940s. Congrats, little sister, I do believe you may have found the pot at the end of the rainbow."

Excitedly, the men began to dig and pull apart the doors to the entrance. Once they opened it, they gave the old mine room to breathe so to speak. Taking the torches they'd brought with them, they stepped into the mine, Desi looking to make sure the supports were still in place.

"See?" she said, "Some of these are a lot newer than they should be. And these bolting mechanisms weren't available until the forties."

Leaving one man at the entrance, the others proceeded cautiously into the mine, almost stumbling upon two well-preserved skeletons, each with a hole in the back of their skulls. They all looked to Gabriella.

"My guess? Either Nazis or locals they made help

them, then killed to keep the secret. Bastards. In the end the SS officers didn't trust anyone but other SS officers. They were afraid of being betrayed. Can't blame them for that… I mean you can blame them for their atrocities before and after the war, but their paranoia was justified."

The cavern shaft split into two. "Which one?" asked Anders as both were blocked from what appeared to be two cave-ins.

"This one," said Desi, pointing to the left.

"How can you be so sure?" asked Nils.

Desiree's smile could have lit up the whole damn mine. "Because while the one on the right was probably blown up to seal the entrance, the one on the left was strategically and structurally created to resemble it. If you look closely, you can see the beams and rocks were hand placed. You don't want to seal your treasure in a place you can't get to it."

Looking where Desi pointed, Gabriella could see she was right. "Damn, sister mine, you're even better than I thought you were."

They began pulling away debris and working together to clear the entrance. As Desi had predicted, the beams, dirt and rocks were merely camouflage for a stout metal vault door. They had anticipated some kind of locking mechanism, but it appeared to be two doors simply chained with a stout lock.

"Cut the chain, not the lock," said Gabriella.

"Why?" asked Berg.

"The Nazis were infamous for booby trapping locks with sulphuric acid. They set them up so if you tried to knock them open or shoot them, they would spray that stuff all over you—sometimes killing the person and sometimes only blinding them. Needless to say, we'd like to avoid that. Cut the chain and handle that lock with great care."

Berg cut through the chain and Anders removed his sweater to wrap around and move the lock to a safe distance. As he returned, Gabriella couldn't help but admire once again his cut chest and eight-pack abs. Her mate was, as her old granny used to say, a 'fine figure of a man.'

They pulled open the doors and Anders and Nils walked in, holding their torches up above and in front of them. Gabriella, Desiree, and Berg followed close behind.

"Oh my God, Gabi, you did it," exclaimed Desiree.

"I think I really did," Gabriella said, feeling her smile grow broader by the minute. "Shit, Anders, we found it."

"No, my beloved, you found it. The rest of us just helped you to break in."

"Is this all of it?" said Nils walking to the back of the shaft.

It was markedly different from the remainder of the mine. Its walls were lined with shelves set into solid armor plating and the floors were made of stone rather than dirt and gravel. The shelves were covered with dusty boxes and long forgotten tools while the floor was littered with square objects draped in canvas cloths.

Gabriella nodded. "Probably, but we'll need a proper team up here. It's long been suspected that the haul was separated and hidden in different places. Let me look to see if I can find what brought us here, at the very least."

They began carefully opening crate after crate of paintings.

Finally, Anders called out. "I think I was after the wrong one," he said, holding up Leon Wyczółkowski's Study – The Bust of a Young Woman. "Tell Zofia if she'd like to sell, I will pay her asking price and it will hang proudly in Sabu. It's stunning."

Gabriella nodded. "I think so, too."

"Let's gather what we can and head back to the chopper," said Anders.

"We should probably leave the treasure here and put it in the hands of the authorities," said Gabriella.

"We'll leave three of the men here to guard the treasure and call Zofia's husband to tell them what we found. Between the police in Bergen and my own men, we should be able to secure and transport the treasure."

"The cops are going to be inclined to call in the experts to document everything."

Anders nodded. "They can do as they wish, but

the finder's fee belongs to Gabriella. If need be, we can hold the treasure at Sabu."

Gabriella laughed. "No, babe, they're going to have a whole team of art historians, archeologists, historians. This is going to be big… huge. They'll most likely just set up camp. We can offer them support, but once the authorities get involved, it'll become a clusterfuck of competing egos. But let's take the Wyczółkowski. I'd like to hand it over to Zofia."

Anders smiled. "We can fly into town. You can give Zofia her family's painting, and I will let her husband know about the find."

They returned to the chopper and sent one more man back to the mine so that four of them were there. Anders promised to call Sabu and send more men in the smaller chopper. They would also send food, drink, and camping provisions.

The chopper lifted off and Anders called and arranged for back up and supplies and arms to be taken up to the mine. They flew down into the town of Bergen, and after calling in a few favors, the street where the Bendera house was located was cleared and the chopper set down to great fanfare.

Before anyone could stop her, Gabriella hopped out with the painting and met Zofia at the gate to their front yard.

"Gabriella? What are you doing here?" she asked.

"And what are you doing with Anders Jensen?" asked her husband suspiciously.

"Zofia," said Gabriella, ignoring him. "I found it."

"Oh, my God," said Zofia, her knees buckling. Anders was closer and leaped the low fence, catching her before she crumbled to the ground. She turned to look at her husband, who seemed unsure what to do. "You really found it?"

Gabriella nodded. "Along with a lot of other stuff. But you have all the documentation you'll need to claim it. They may want to take it for a while, but I wanted you to at least be able to touch it and see it."

She handed the twenty-seven by twenty-two centimeter painting to Zofia, who held it as if it was a priceless treasure. To her, it was.

"I would say you don't know what this means, but I know you do."

Gabriella nodded. "I do."

Anders looked at Zofia's husband. "Gabriella found a cache of Nazi treasure. I have my men up there, but to keep it secure is going to take a lot of manpower and Gabriella says Interpol has a whole unit set up for this."

Bendera nodded. "They do." He extended his hand to Anders. "I cannot thank you enough. This means the world to us."

"It was our pleasure. You should know that we think a group of Odessa and bratva are looking for the cache. They tried to kill Gabriella but failed."

Bendera quirked an eyebrow but said nothing. "We'll put the painting in the bank's safe and I will call Interpol and get more men up to supplement yours."

"Good. I have supplies being sent up. If your people will come to my landing strip, we'll take them up."

"That is good. I am at a loss for words," said Bendera.

"None are needed, but if you decide to sell it, I would be honored to buy it."

Bendera said nothing but inclined his head.

∽

One Month Later
Sabu Stronghold

Friends, family, and invited guests stood in the foyer of the Sabu Stronghold to admire Wyczółkowski's Study – The Bust of a Young Woman where it now hung in a place of honor. It truly was a beautiful piece. Zofia had decided that her family could use the money and that it would be far safer at Sabu than at her house. Anders had been able to buy it for a fair price with the promise that he would let it be displayed at the Louvre when the exhibit of the found pieces went on tour.

Interpol's art investigation team had done an outstanding job of documenting the find at the site and then transporting all of the pieces, minus the Wyczółkowski, to their headquarters in Lyon. The drawing of the lioness had not been among the pieces recovered and Gabriella had made a vow to find it. She wouldn't allow Anders to simply add it to his collection, but she would afford him the opportunity, at least, to buy it. Because, as Gabriella had predicted, Zofia had exceptional documentation and Gabriella's independent research had verified it, she was given the painting to do with as she wished. Luckily for Anders, that had been to sell it to him.

They were throwing a party, partially to celebrate their wedding. Her parents and brother had been surprised and then delighted when Gabriella had called to announce she was marrying Anders. They had done so as the sun rose over the eastern horizon and celebrated with an intimate gathering for lunch. The much larger reception and party to celebrate the acquisition of the painting had been planned for that same evening.

There was music, laughter, dancing, and just an air of love and joy in the air. It was everything Gabriella could have wanted to celebrate her bonding to Anders. Anders had been busy playing host and making nice to her brother, who was coming around to the idea that maybe having a brother-in-law with the kind of clout and money that Anders had might not be such a bad thing.

Desi had just left her to dance with Nils when Gabriella felt Anders near, smiling as he slipped his arm around her.

"You have outdone yourself," he whispered, nuzzling her neck. "Happy?"

"Very much."

"What are you thinking?"

"Aside from how much I want to get out of this dress and make mad, passionate love to you?"

He chuckled. "Yes, aside from that. I cannot simply abscond with you into my study, toss you onto the desk, ruck up your skirts, open my fly, and have at you."

"No? I thought you once told me you were alpha, and your word is law."

Anders laughed and swatted her backside. "Unless your mother is here," he confided. "In which case, all defer to her."

Gabriella leaned into her handsome mate and lifted her champagne glass to him. As they clinked glasses, she whispered, "*La de gode tidene rulle.*"

EPILOGUE

"He killed my sister," snarled Rhys Donovan, slamming her fist down on the desk of the head of Interpol's office in Stockholm. "God damn it! Do something."

"Ms. Donovan, as I've explained, I can neither confirm nor deny your sister's ever having worked with or for Interpol, nor do I even have any confirmation of a Maeve Donovan's death or disappearance. In fact, the only reason I know someone by that name ever lived is you have presented me with her birth certificate. I am doing you the courtesy of not questioning its validity."

Had this asshole just called her a liar?

"Listen," she snarled, looking at the nameplate on his desk, "Mr. Gustafsson. Wait is your first name really Kermitt? Kermitt Gustafsson? Did your mother have a difficult labor? Or maybe she adopted you and you're the love child of Kermit the Frog and the Swedish Chef. That must be it."

"There's no reason to be insulting, Ms. Donovan," he said in a huffy tone.

Now that she looked at him, Rhys had to admit, he kind of looked like a Kermitt Gustafsson. And what was with the Swedes and all the weird double consonants? Did they and the Welsh have something in common? A language looking to buy a vowel?

"I see every reason. You people convinced my sister that you needed her help to get Lars Jakobsson. And now she is dead, or at best missing, and you people want to play games to cover your ass and protect your operation. Well, I'm sorry, that doesn't work for me. If you won't do anything, I will."

Rhys turned around, prepared to leave his office and go find her sister. She had no idea how she was going to do that, but she was either going to find Maeve or crucify whoever had killed her. As far as she could tell, Lars Jakobsson was her primary suspect. A known mafia kingpin, he was the head of the Berserker Syndicate. Pfft, ever since the popularity of the show, everybody and their brother was claiming to be a descendant of Vikings. Well, maybe he was. Rhys didn't give a damn.

Willing her tears back, Rhys threw open the door, only to be confronted by another man in an ill-fitting, bland suit, barring her exit.

"Get out of my way," she snarled.

"Ms. Donovan," called Kermitt, "I'm afraid I can't let you leave in this state. Rolff, please close the door."

Rolff—she was sure his name had two Fs—reached for the handle. Feeling alone, vulnerable, and worried for her sister, Rhys knew she couldn't expect any help from these people and that there was a very real possibility she'd be booted out of the country. That would add a degree of difficulty in finding her sister that she didn't need.

"Rolff," she said in warning. "Move it or lose it. Kermitt isn't going to punch you if you don't comply, but I will."

She waited. The smug, self-satisfied smile sealed his doom. Looking him straight in the eye, Rhys punched him in the nuts, making him squeal like a pig and drop like a stone. She didn't wait to see Kermitt's reaction, she just ran for the door, bolting past the elevator and down the stairs. Rhys could hear shouting behind her and the banging of the stairwell door as they gave chase. She'd seen a skybridge linking this building to the one across the street on the third floor.

Darting through the door onto the third floor, she made a mad dash for the door to the skybridge. God love the Swedes and their arrogance about having a low crime rate. Interior doors to stairwells and exits were rarely locked as long as the building itself was open. Dashing down the hall, she rushed through the door and made herself walk across the skybridge, trotting down the external stairs onto the street below, before blending in with the crowd.

She smiled, hearing the shouts and venting frustration at her having eluded them. Thankfully, she had already stopped by Maeve's flat and taken all of her papers, her laptop, and several items of no real value other than to Maeve. Those swinging against her hip in her satchel, she made her way to the closest car rental agency, rented a Volvo and merged into the traffic, exiting the city in an orderly fashion.

Once she cleared the city limits, and no one was close enough behind her to see what she was doing in the car, she raised her fist and shot Stockholm her happy middle finger.

"Fuck you, Stockholm."

ACKNOWLEDGMENTS

Thank you to my Patreon supporters.
I couldn't do this without you!

Carol Chase
Latoya McBride
Julia Rappaport
D F
Ellen
Margaret Bloodworth
Tamara Crooks
Rhonda
Suzy Sawkins
Cindy Vernon
Linda Kniffen-Wager
Karen Somerville

ABOUT DELTA JAMES

Other books by Delta James: https://www.deltajames.com/

As a USA Today bestselling romance author, Delta James aims to captivate readers with stories about complex heroines and the dominant alpha males who adore them. For Delta, romance is more than just a love story; it's a journey with challenges and thrills along the way.

After creating a second chapter for herself that was dramatically different than the first, Delta now resides in Virginia where she relaxes on warm summer evenings with her lovable pack of basset hounds as they watch the birds of prey soaring overhead and the fireflies dancing in the fading light. When not crafting fast-paced tales, she enjoys horseback riding, hiking, and white-water rafting.

Her readers mean the world to her, and Delta tries to interact personally to as many messages as she can. If you'd like to chat or discuss books, you can find Delta on Instagram, Facebook, and in her private reader group https://www.facebook.com/groups/348982795738444.

If you're looking for your next bingeable series, you can get a FREE story by joining her newsletter https://www.subscribepage.com/VIPlist22019.

ALSO BY DELTA JAMES

Syndicate Masters: Northern Lights

Alliance

Complication

Judgement

Syndicate Masters

The Bargain

The Pact

The Agreement

The Understanding

Masters of Valor

Prophecy

Illusion

Deception

Inheritance

Masters of the Savoy

Advance

Negotiation

Submission

Contract

Bound

Release

Fated Legacy

Touch of Fate

Touch of Darkness

Touch of Light

Touch of Fire

Touch of Ice

Touch of Destiny

Masters of the Deep

Silent Predator

Fierce Predator

Savage Predator

Wicked Predator

Ghost Cat Canyon

Determined

Untamed

Bold

Fearless

Strong

Boxset

Tangled Vines

Corked

Uncorked

Decanted

Breathe

Full Bodied

Late Harvest

Boxset 1

Boxset 2

Mulled Wine

Wild Mustang

Hampton

Mac

Croft

Noah

Thom

Reid

Box Set #1

Box Set #2

Wayward Mates

In Vino Veritas

Brought to Heel

Marked and Mated

Mastering His Mate

Taking His Mate

Claimed and Mated

<u>Claimed and Mastered</u>

<u>Hunted and Claimed</u>

<u>Captured and Claimed</u>

Printed in Great Britain
by Amazon